All over the world the whales were coming ashore, in a ritual mass suicide that no species of animal had ever matched. In the laboratories of Tokyo, at the secret police headquarters of Moscow, beside the Big Dish at Arecibo that peered blindly into space for another voice, even among the motorcycle gangs and ordinary citizens of California the phenomenon brought an astonished question: *Why?*

And the answer—

Because they have tasted men's minds, and they are dying of it . . .

Bantam Books by Ian Watson

THE EMBEDDING
THE JONAH KIT

the jonah kit

by Ian Watson

RLI: VLM 9 (VLR 9–10)
IL 8+

THE JONAH KIT
*A Bantam Book / published by arrangement with
Charles Scribner's Sons*

PRINTING HISTORY
Scribner's edition published April 1976
Bantam edition / February 1978

ISBN 0-553-10879-4

ich spreche von euerm nicht,
ich spreche vom ende der eulen.
ich spreche von butt und wal . . .
ich spreche nicht mehr von euch,
planern der spurlosen tat . . .
ich spreche von dem was nicht spricht,
von den sprachlosen zeugen . . .

i do not speak of what's yours,
i speak of the end of owls.
i speak of turbot and whale . . .
i don't speak of you any more,
planners of vanishing actions . . .
i speak of that without speech,
of the unspeaking witnesses . . .

—Hans Magnus Enzensberger
    (translated by Michael Hamburger)

To Jessica

One

He swims across a mountain range. The razorback peaks rise abruptly from the bottom ooze, enclosing dank zigzagging canyons in any one of which a great cunning Ten-Arms might be skulking with its ripping suckers and arms tough as steel . . .

But why mention steel?

Smooth and rigid, Steel encloses empty spaces resembling intestines, stomachs, and lungs, which aren't any of these things since they never respond to the world about them by the slightest shape-changing.

Steel hasn't anything to do with Ten-Arms. Unless there's a Steel he hasn't come across yet, that can writhe and twist and change its shape! Tough as steel is . . . a metaphor. A way of knowing.

What a weak, unsound way!

He compares his mental model of a Ten-Arms reaching up to wrap suckers round his forehead—a painful memory, this!—with one of a Steel cruising a deep trench: a pregnant Steel, with a dozen steel fetuses upright in womb pods along her back. (Cu-

1

riously rigid and lifeless, though, her little ones—for all that there's a tiny heart tick present in each of them . . . !)

The complex sound-pictures grate against each other; there's no correspondence.

So why is it in him, this metaphor urge?

On the fringes of his consciousness exists a blur, a foggy wall that he's familiar with the existence of, but baffled by its nature. It isn't memory as he understands memory; still, it has something of memory about it; for the hundredth time his mind claws at this fog . . .

. . . till he feels fingers (which he doesn't possess) touching the clammy *steel* of an enormous tank, inside which he is somehow also present, as a prisoner. . . . These fingers slide along like blind worms till they're too numb to feel. They freeze and fall off one by one, till there never were any fingers, and there's only a crawling sensation of lampreys on his skin—finger-parasites wavering as he swims, rasping ulcers in his hide with their stinging, slobber mouths . . .

He circles the mountain peaks, waist muscles contracting, tail rising and falling, flukes pivoting on the upstroke and the down in a sensual forward thrust —his whole body copulating with these waters as he swims, thrusting himself again and again into a pliable yielding softness that parts for him, and parts; his penis itself staying inert, recessed—irrelevant to this grand intercourse with the medium of his existence.

Yet his copulatory thrust carries within it the weak echo of an earlier sensation—hint of a time when his tail blades were forked far wider apart than now; when the underside of his body squirmed upon the soft warmth of some other clinging, shifting being; and all along his spine was bitter cold; and it was black dark everywhere. . . . A residue of strange joy, and fear, clings to him, lampreylike. . . .

He searches peaks and canyons far below, building

himself an exact sound model of the crags and depths, the water density gradients, deep scattering layers of crustaceans, jellyfish, siphonophores, that billow out around the mountains in faint veils. A percussion of croaks, drummings, and grunts stipples his echo map, too, from other small food beasts making noises.

Finally, he raises his head to eye the sky-barrier undulating right and left.

Monotonous rubbery contortions, rippling . . .

His eyesight's such a poor weak partial thing—it casts so little light on what he hears; hardly tells him anything at all.

Yet there's a queer sense of miracle in seeing this bending luminous web—this thing of light . . . no nagging ghosts cling to it. It seems freshly created for him every moment.

He surely pays it more attention than it deserves—for what's a sky, but just a place to gulp air, and blow? Yet he cannot shake his delight in its visibility. He could hear well enough—with perfect pitch—even before he came into the sea. . . . But light is new.

Came *into?*

But he must always have swum the seas—else his great body would have crushed itself to death!

Tang of his own urine tells him he has cruised full circle and crossed his tracks. Distinct, too, dissolving feces of Sweetmeats that passed this way a short while ago. Their drifting flakes of dung trigger a hungry memory of sweet, oily flesh in his mouth. . . . How pungently he can taste this sea world! How tangibly he can click-map it!

He'd been going to die once, he realizes. But he didn't die. Instead, he's here.

Cruising. Copulating with the sea. Mapping this world of waters. Occasionally thrusting himself through the sky's soft roof to spill out numbers that seem to grow in him spontaneously—forcing out feces of the mind, before diving deep to safety.

And all the time rasped by ghosts . . .

Two

"The Nilin boy's run away," Professor Kapelka told
Katya Tarsky as she entered his office to make her
daily report. He said it in such an abrupt, startled
chirrup that she felt she had burst in on some private
conversation. She glanced round the room, but there
was no one else there; then at the cradled telephone.
Following the drift of her eyes, Kapelka's scrawny
avian hand made a vague gesture of reaching for the
phone, but he didn't carry the action through, and
looked at his watch instead.

"Yes, absconded," he repeated. "The most I can give
our own people to find him is another hour."

His fingernails scuttled away from the black Bake-
lite instrument, across the mahogany expanse of his
desk, and began pecking away at the same spot rep-
etitively. The desk was a czarist antique from some
old mansion or other. It had wormholes in it, and Kapelka looked as though he was trying to drum up
some long-ago fumigated, petrified worm from one of
them.

"I shall have to notify the supervisory committee

after that. . . . Oh, this could deal a terrible blow to our project, Katya!"

"But why? If he's only run off playing truant in the hills, surely it's only a question of time? The weather's warm enough. The boy can't come to harm—"

She gestured indignantly at the outside world.

The professor's window faced inland across a scattering of wooden buildings with tall, smoking chimneys, up sloping meadows of dry grass hedged by bamboo thickets and conifer groves that progressively thickened into forest the further inland you went. The first snow had fallen a few days earlier—then melted as the weather warmed again, unseasonably. Several white pockets still gleamed. Probably they wouldn't melt till next summer. Still, the weather bureau said this warm spell might last a week or more.

Her gaze fell short of the forests and meadows, rooting itself upon one particular smoking building of two stories where the boy was housed. Or, had been housed . . .

The research center had preempted practically the whole sea frontage and harbor of the township of Ozerskiy, displacing the small herring cannery which had been here before. With only one small village further south toward the peninsula, and lacking any rail link northward to Korsakov with its shipyards, lumber mills, and fur plants, Ozerskiy was a lonely spot, yet drably beautiful, too, with its cold clean air, long snowfalls, lashing summer rain.

That house was also where . . .

But the thought pained her. The man kept in there wasn't really Pavel Chirikov at all! The real Pavel had died, mentally. Leaving twin ghosts behind him . . . One, animating the body in that building in a purely zombie fashion. The other, a mathematical abstraction, that swam a mile down . . . Neither was the actual Pavel. Any other attitude was madness. (And yet. And yet!)

"No, you see, Katya, the attendant has run away, too. They stole a boat. Well, a boat has gone . . . I don't suppose it's a coincidence. If we don't find them ourselves, we'll have far less freedom in future. We'll be supervised much more directly—the whole experiment, I imagine. . . ."

"But why should that matter, professor? The project is *valid!* It's proving itself already, wonderfully!"

Her eyes shone: glossy black stones set in tired, turbid gray pools.

The old man, with the birdlike features of a wizard in a fairy story (which indeed he was to her—a magician who could unpick the maze of a man's mind) regarded his young assistant sadly. Her crinkly black hair swept back through a whalebone ring that splayed out an unkempt bush down the back of her blue overalls—like the Rusalka of legends, he thought, the drowned girl who became a water spirit —with uncombed, disheveled hair . . . yet it wasn't she who had gone underwater. Once again, he wished he could say out loud to her: *"Devushka Rusalka—* lady water spirit, why can't you fall in love again, with someone else, and forget, forget. . . ." He knew where she'd been staring; knew which window. Knew that it wasn't because of the boy's absence. Yet the nearest he ever really came to voicing that level of intimacy was his constant use of her familiar name, as to a daughter. Besides, when she could perform her job so exhaustively well, and so intuitively, while half-mesmerized by this ghastly passion of hers—wasn't it silly to intervene and destroy this?

So, instead, he lectured her:

"Ah, but what is valid in the eyes of military men, and politicians, Katya? Dividends! In terms of war— the problem of the deep-submergence submarine, that can roost on its brood of missiles so quietly a kilometer beneath the waves. How to track it. How to trap it. Even more valid, perhaps—since the nuclear war might never be fought, pray God, but the economic war surely must be—control of the wealth of the oceans. The oil wells. The manganese nodules. All the fuel and minerals for the future. He who holds the key to the deep seabed holds the future world in his palm. Equally, he who can interfere with another's control—by the use of a Jonah, or any other means— has a gun to point at other heads. Did you know that the Americans have a plan for *ten-kilometer-wide* tripods on the deep seabed, to listen out for submarines? How many of *these* dividends is the project reaping so far? So few, Katya! There are men of hard fact out there. And all over the world men of hard fact are growing frightened these days—at the drying-up wells, at the emptying mines. We have had freedom such as I never dared dream of as a young researcher, up till now. Because ours was truly a creative dream, and the men of hard fact had the sense to see we needed freedom to put our dream to work. But the committee is asking so many questions lately. How soon, how soon, is their dividend! Before we can put our model into production! How cost-effective is it? How efficient will it be? Oh, all the jargon of capitalism, Katya! Oh, yes, as in America, so here! And ours seems to be such a mental experiment, still. . . . Almost, a spiritual dream! So I say to them how we have to test our system out. I explain how much more complex it is than any new aircraft or spacecraft, this seacraft of ours. I have to put it in these mechanical terms, Katya," he apologized, noticing the hurt on her face.

He drew breath.

"I even accuse them of loss of nerve. Like the Americans—retreating from space, when they could have grasped it. . . . They don't like that, Katya. But now the boy's disappearance makes a fool of us. How can we control a far-off Jonah when we can't keep one little boy in check? That is the sum of it. One boy, who is also, remember . . ." He tailed off, leaving the rest unsaid, and pecked again at his desk.

"I believe we are going to find something wonderful out soon, professor," the dark-haired girl affirmed. "Something unexpected. Something awe-inspiring."

"Ah, but what, Katya? And, as they say to me, how soon?"

Intuition? She could be right, he thought. Her torment—bound up with a passionate joy while she continued believing in their Jonah—kept her on such a knife-edge of insight and empathy as sometimes seemed almost weird, unnatural. . . .

"What is it like down there, for him?" she mused, fiercely, disregarding his question. "Every word we use betrays *his* experience. How does he tell the difference between the giant squid and the octopus he meets? What music is he singing now, to map them?"

Kapelka shrugged, reasonably.

"He has a radar in his head, Katya—a natural radar. He hears the shapes. Well, squids are decapods, aren't they? So he hears ten-tentacled torpedos. And octopuses look more like sea spiders with their eight limbs. I suppose they sound that way, too. Then there'll be emotional overtones—or reflexes—because an octopus is just a harmless foodstuff, while a really giant squid can kill him. The octopus echo should have a benign ring to it. . . . Now what's this about something unexpected?"

Before Katya could answer him, the phone jangled.

"You see," she smiled, as Kapelka raised the receiver, "they've found him. It's all right."

Kapelka shook his head as he listened.

Recradling the receiver, he said sadly, "They're out in the strait by now. There's a fog coming up over the water! This idiot weather! Of course, they'll run out of fuel. . . . But they could drift halfway to Japan before the fog lifts. So I'll have to call the coast guard. Which means that everybody knows. Save your surprises till later, Katya. Come and make your report this evening. Maybe you can bring some joy. . . ."

Three

Overtaken by uncertainty, confusion, fright, he blows a spout of oily foam from his single nostril and lies on the surface, gasping air—his model of the mountains below him blurring as he wallows idiotically in spume, haunted by touches he can't have felt, by a body he never owned, by notions of noises conveying urgent meanings by way of mouth . . . Isolated and inefficient, the troughs of ocean toss him then for minute after minute.

He knows his own body well—the flex of his jaws, the waft of his flukes, how the melon of his great brow walls in its flexible maze of valves and passages aflow with waxy oil. Yet it's as though he's only steersman in a vast Steel made of flesh!

A nightmare image of this steersman attacks him now. A cunning Eight-Arms, such as nests on the rocky ledges of the cliffs below, is nesting in his mind —its tentacles playing tricks with his thoughts, its suckers operating them one by one; with its sharp beak ready to peck a hole in his melon wall and empty him out, if his thoughts think back too far . . .

Inside his neck, behind his neck, somewhere—where he can't ever see it or hear it, but only feel its tentacles, and its beak, tickling him first, then scratching, then ripping sadistically—lives this Eight-Arms. Once a day it wakes up, gorged on "numbers," and bullies him.

He cruises in pandemonium, burst-pulsing chaotically, loading his melon with ill-structured mush from the waves, almost the echo of a cry of distress; and just while he is acting in this most senseless way, the beak begins to peck at him. The itch starts urging him.

Eight-Arms in his mind has awakened. In its slumber it was counting out numbers of the suckers that clung to his thoughts while he mapped the sea-floor, and Steels, in the click-pulse way of his mind.

While it sleeps, he can forget about it. It disappears below the surface. Only the lampreys of memory sting him then. But now he has to communicate his itch, to send it to sleep again. He has to avoid its meal of numbers in the air above the waters.

So he rolls about in the ocean troughs, gathering himself, then humping his body higher, his eyes squint out myopically above the fretted, spray-torn waste his roof of rubber light is, from above; and the Eight-Arms inside him presents numbers that he can send—a set of clicks dispersing uselessly into the empty air. . . . But he doesn't question this, as he pulses. The need is too urgent.

In another hour he'll hear clicks inside his head, in his neck, somewhere. With Eight-Arms' help he'll understand them. Then Eight-Arms can go to sleep again, counting in his sleep . . . and he'll be free for another day.

Between now and that moment, though, the panic fear that a blow might strike him from the air! The flight to safety—!

He hyperoxygenates the hemoglobin in his blood, the myoglobin in his muscles—then lobtails abruptly, flipping his flukes high above the surface and stand-

ing on his brow in the sea for a brief moment before
diving deep.

What is this blow he fears?
A fist of steel, delivered from the air . . .
And a "fist" is fingers coiled up in a ball to break
his bones and stave his skull in. Fingers are small
Steels standing erect inside a Mother Steel . . .
But this solves nothing; this is still mysterious. How
can he explain it to his own kind? They hear him
clicking at the air. They hear the foreign clicking in
his head. He has been naïve enough to ask their help.
To pulse questions at them. About this; and the ghosts
on the fringes of his consciousness.
Their own messages are sagas of action against
the Great Ten-Arms of the Sea, praise songs of bulls,
laments at the death of females in labor, love songs;
then, increasingly abstract and hard for him to grasp,
those idea maps culminating in the Star Glyphs, the
High Philosophy of his kind.
At first he provoked sympathy, condolences for a
sickness; once, aversion and flight; now latterly, a
piercing, mounting interest.
Perhaps they can help him after all.

He plunges, and realizes his error only as cliffs
race up to meet him. Jagged, eroded crags pen him
in amongst them. Yet his dive seems inevitable; he
cannot turn back. Downward he goes, the pressure
collapsing his lungs against pliable ribs, his heartbeat
slowing and the blood flow cutting off from most of
his organs. As his temperature falls, the oil in his
brow congeals to a harder wax, weighing him down
and becoming an even finer echo screen.
And all the echoes from around his plunging body
warn of a perilous tunnel of heaped crags with razor
edges!
Yet his tail drives him downward as fiercely as
ever into the slit of the canyon.
Hitting one ledge of lava, crumbling it, driving

knives into his hide, he ricochets towards another wall of fire ...

He passes through veils of comb jellies, arrowworms and glassworms hanging in soft crystalline blankets; through schools of silver darters; then through brown medusae, redworms and violet pteropods at the furthest reach of the light—but his eyes pay no heed to any of them; nor to any stray phosphorescences generating their own light down in the black below the light. And despite the precision with which his hardened wax prints every echo, tangible as the tooth buds in his lower jaw, prints every nodule sprouting from the bottom ooze, he still slams into this, jarring himself violently. He hangs a moment, brow buried in mud, before righting himself and pitching his way, half-deaf, through the narrow cracks between the cliffs, twisting right, twisting left, barely avoiding collisions.

Flight!
He was trotting in fear, stumbling over cold, soft hummocks, bruising himself when he sprawled, but rising and trotting on breathlessly—till thin "fingers" whipped him to a halt ...

A "voice" pursued him: arbitrary sounds approaching meaning, like waves on a shoreline, only to fall back in nonsensical jangle—"words" somehow associated with the joyful squirming of his body, with the "smell" of hair flowing under him like weed.

Was he fleeing from dying? But he had dying within him ...

Perhaps he was fleeing from joy?

Yet how he fled, breaching on limbs he knows nothing of, performing for minute after minute the jumping dance upon the surface of the sea that always brings him crashing back below, in seconds!

He'd been able to balance in air, light and frail as a jellyfish. ...

Had that been his "soul," then, before he existed?

If only they can penetrate the vortex of this madness! Or he will surely destroy himself.

He thinks of this Being in him as an Eight-Arms, after the model of the Eight-Arms he has seen nesting on cliffs, manipulating the world with their tentacles—and eaten up sometimes, catching them out in the open water. His relation to it is ambiguous. It feeds him mentally, he senses; yet manipulates him, hurts him, too. . . . It is Him, and Not-Him. He can't feel the pure opposition that the Great Ten-Arms generates in him—who battles him physically in the seaworld deeps, whom he can physically defeat. . . . The Eight-Arms in him is Another Self, along another axis of being. Every actual Eight-Arms that he chomps in his jaws and swallows down, he dedicates to it tactfully, propitiatingly. . . .

He has cruised half his allotted time, has calmed and is registering more accurately where he is heading, when he rounds a buttress and there, head-on in the narrow canyon, finds facing him a Ten-Arm Intelligence, full-grown to his own length, and alert. . . .

Four

On Monday afternoon, Paul Hammond unexpectedly decreed a half-day holiday from the hectic radio observations of the past few weeks for himself and Richard Kimble, and suggested they should drive down with Ruth and Baby Alice to watch the gray whales migrating north.

Richard regarded the invitation with some suspicion, being well aware of Paul's lofty contempt for his amateur interest in whales—not to mention Paul's likely awareness of Richard's faltering, equivocal affair with Ruth Hammond.

As it turned out, though, it was internal politics he wanted to talk about—particularly Max Berg's opposition to the histrionic manner Paul seemed set on announcing their findings in. Whales—and Ruth—were only sweeteners for the pill.

So they drove down the long, winding unmade road from the radio dish after lunch in Paul's station wagon, a Sierra, heading for the cliffs beyond San Pedro de la Paz.

The dish itself resembled a cross between a giant

stylized ear and a pair of hands cupped for hallooing;
and as they left, a group of the local Mezapico Indians stood whistling up at it, nodding approvingly
as echoes rebounded. That's how to do it! their ex-
pressions seemed to say—as though the Americans
had failed to bring the giant machine to life properly.
It could move about in a restricted circuit, like a
tethered goat—but it was dumb.

Their whistles were, in fact, how Richard had
learned that the gray whale migration was on. Since
yesterday, the Mezapico had been whistling the
news up the mountain. A wizened odd-job man had
told him what it meant—and he mentioned it to
Paul, hardly expecting this sudden picnic excursion
to result.

Paul Hammond glanced at the Indians uncurious-
ly, dismissing them into the same limbo as the kites
and vultures perched on the support spars of the dish
—neither Indians nor wild birds made the least difference to the microwave radiation from the stars.
His electric shock of hair swept back in the breeze
of driving. It was grown just long enough, and wild
enough, to signify inspiration without eccentricity.
His eyes appeared bright and obsessive—but contrived to look wise, too: as though he was wearing
some sort of interior contact lenses, composed of sa-
gacity—a kind of intellectual converse of cataracts.
His firm ambery flesh belied his age—past forty. "He
does isometrics in the starlight before he comes to
bed," Ruth had said sarcastically.

Traditionally, scientists have their Great Idea by
the time they are thirty and spend the rest of their
life building on it. Dr. Paul Hammond had made
his breakthrough somewhat tardily, at thirty-five,
with his discovery of the colliding, smaller partner
galaxy to our own, duly named Hammond, hidden
beyond the dust clouds and stars on the farther side
of the Galactic core, and responsible for the periodic
shudders running through the Milky Way, hitherto
identified as gravity waves, and now regarded as a
radically different phenomenon—Topological Catas-

trophe, or Hammond Waves. That had stirred up
sufficient publicity worldwide, Richard recalled wryly
—panic about colliding galaxies. . . . Hammond became a household name, for a while. Now he seemed
bent on making up for lost time and winning a double
crown, and had left such local issues as galaxies far
behind.

"We need to make a big splash with this one—toss a
boulder in the pond! Look at the problem of funds
for one thing, Richard. They've canceled just about
everything else. So many particle accelerators and
space probes down the sink. We'll show the bastards.
The biggest breakthrough in basic knowledge of the
universe. But I want to be sure we present a unified
front. I need active backing from Max, not just some
form of tacit consent."

The Sierra ground through Mezapico village, scattering chickens among the adobe huts, tin shacks,
and slightly more substantial brick and tile buildings
—among which were a shabby bar, a few shops and
private dwellings of the richer peasantry, a lottery
office, and a police station. Some laborers were re-
building the front wall of the latter, which one of the
supply trucks for the telescope had swerved into a
few days before. A row of iron bars grinned through
the gap, behind which someone hunkered in the
gloom wrapped in a sarape.

Old women stared at them blankly from faces as
fissured as the cerebral hemispheres of the brain.
Their skulls had split in the heat and been peeled off
to hang as mementi mori in the little Mezapico church,
whose tower shoved up its single bell at the street's
end: a solitary eyeball set in a long chalk face, surveying the baked, tattered village with resignation.

"Remember that day we went in there, Rich?" Ruth
remarked moodily, while Paul wrestled to avoid a
dog—she'd noted the quick smug look he gave her
and Richard when he used the phrase "tacit consent."
"While I was pregnant. . . . So damn greasy," she
shuddered. "Wax on the seats, everywhere. Like in-

side a honeycomb. I guess all the candle smoke settles."

"I thought they'd been polishing the seats."

"What on earth for?"

"Devotion? Like we arrange flowers in church?"

"Only there aren't any flowers," she laughed, "just sticks and thorns. What a dump."

Richard gazed at the bell as Paul drove toward it, tapping his fingers on the steering wheel impatiently. Its faint daily tinklings for mass percolated up through the still air as far as the observatory. At least it could make some noise! While the great dish on the hill was a monument to deafness—clapper pointed rigidly at the sky in prosthetic erection. . . . The church bell copied the radio dish in absurd, inverted miniature.

Naked brown children tossed pebbles at the station wagon in a fitful way without bothering to take aim, to repay it for its cloud of dust. The village priest hovered outside his church, squinting dubiously at the vehicle and its passengers. For no special reason, not knowing the man, Ruth waved at him and shouted, "Hi there, *buenas tardes!*" Then the ruts and bumps got worse and woke Alice. The baby flushed pink, threatening a squall.

In the backyards of the last few buildings, younger women were kneeling among wandering dogs and hens at waist looms—a couple of sticks stuck in the soil with the warp threads stretched between them— weaving bright zany zigzag cloth from threads others were spinning on hand spindles as simply constructed as the looms were—they were just crude shafts with wooden discs as flywheels. One fat lady with her black braids knotted up around the back of her head superintended the oil drums used to contain the dyes.

Baby Alice flapped her hands violently, banging them against the door handle, her mother's body, Richard's arm. They were sitting three abreast on the long front seat, at Paul's insistence—he didn't like having to talk over his shoulder to people.

"Gentle, Ally, gentle," crooned Ruth, cuddling her daughter up against her shirt, making the button nipples of her small tight breasts stand out against the fabric as though she had the garment on inside out.

Alice seemed bent on maximizing every lurch and jolt of the Sierra in protest at the shaking around she was getting. She opened her mouth wide as a newly hatched birdchick. But it wasn't to cry. Or demand food. It was to yawn—implosively, in total abrupt boredom.

Ruth grimaced sidelong at Richard. One of Paul's tricks, this sudden yawn. An active, functional yawn, it was—brisk as a cruel word, or a slap in the face. As used by Paul in meetings.

The hand-flapping, too, was a miniature of Paul's gesticulations. Not to mention the few spiky curls of fair hair that Alice had. When Alice grew older and the rubbery yogurt of her skin had time to tan a little, she'd be the perfect model female Paul.

Ruth had her own special facility for boredom—and had it in plenty, Richard reflected. Yet it acted more like a vacuum cleaner, perpetually sucking experiences into the same tight black bag.

Yet who could blame her? Translate it into a man's terms. Up Alice's age by twenty years. How would it feel for someone marrying this female version of Dr. Paul? A constant put-down of the man's ego. Alice would choose someone whom she could overwhelm when she grew up; who would worship her briefly; but never be brilliant enough for her, so that his job, whatever it was—insurance salesman, lab technician—would always seem derelict and deficient. Maybe he'd go out and get drunk and have furtive abortive affairs to make it up to himself, feeling curdled inside all the while; and even realize that she wanted him this way all along: an empty stage for her own dramas.

Ruth's own hair was black. Not jet-black or ebony-black or any such; but just plain black—though she'd worn it luxuriously long enough when she first met

Paul. Recently, though, she'd cropped it to a spiky helmet. Shorn of the long hair, her face revealed its basic peaky character, that hadn't been so obvious to herself before—though doubtless in retrospect it had always been apparent to the various TV agents and drama school instructors who capitalized on her ambitions. Without enough character to be an actress, and without looks enough to star in commercials, her long, black, assiduously cultivated hair had woven a precarious bridge between two delusions— now she had cut it loose.

The road descended steeply now into Ciudad Juarez past flocks of goats, maize fields, cactus hedges. Ciudad Juarez was a larger town than Mezapico. Its church boasted twin spires and twin bells, with a spacious dusty square opening out before the church— the *zocalo*, a small shrub garden in its center.

A handsome, cheeky-faced Indian youth was squatting on the check-tiled perimeter wall of his garden. He jumped to his feet as they drove round the square counterclockwise, stuffed his fingers in his mouth and emitted a piercing series of whistles. Baby Alice swung her face in his direction and squealed in return twice, experimentally, soaring off the edge of the scale into inaudibility.

"He must take to me," giggled Ruth, as the youth stood watching them while they receded through the dust. His loose homespun *manta* shirt and trousers were ragged, but a bright vermilion sash round his waist gave him a dandyish air.

"We're reaching beyond the end of the universe, eh, Richard?" growled Hammond. "It'll shake 'em. It won't be just some galaxy called Hammond or some Hammond Waves this time—"

"You're not kidding, the end of the universe," Ruth commented bitterly, indicating the scrub, cactus, and stony fields resuming immediately outside the town, a few bent figures hoeing in them.

"I mean the telescope has, obviously, Ruth. We're past the limit of observable stars and galaxies—harking back to the time before they were formed, hearing the echoes of the Big Bang that's supposed to have started it all—"

"Ah yes, your famous 'Footsteps of God'—that's what you call it, isn't it?" Ruth nudged Richard. "See, I know the cues. Paul only has to mention 'Isotropy' or 'Microwave Background,' and I salivate obediently in my head. Still, it isn't the same as *understanding* the script—that's a distinction Paul never seems to grasp. Where does God come into it? The way Paul's carrying on lately, you'd think you were founding a new religion, not just stargazing! 'This is the way the world ends, not with a bang but a whimper,'" she quoted. "'Modern Verse Drama,'" she apologized brightly. "I got a B for the course. On the other hand, what if the world begins with a whimper and ends with a bang?"

"You'd not make that remark unless you understood," Paul pointed out in his unique blend of blandness and acidity. Richard wished fervently they could reach the sea a little faster.

"Did I ever tell you, Rich," Ruth backtracked—whistling the opening bars of a song he was all too familiar with, "I was working my way through drama school when I met Paul in that motel? Study life, that's the Stanislavsky method, isn't it? Someone in theater arts said go work in a motel. I wonder if it was a joke. Meaning I could study being a receptionist—sort of perpetual understudy? Hey-di-hey, there I met Paul—thus the yarrow sticks fell!"

She said no more, but he knew the rest of the recital by heart. How Paul needed an understudy for a wife. How it said something about his manhood. Paul thought Ruth was good in bed—therefore Paul thought *he* was the really good one. But Ruth wasn't much good as a lover. However, Paul didn't notice—so this Laingian knot proceeded—because she couldn't *act* being good at it well enough to expose him. So he was safe, and his self-esteem secure. This self-esteem carried him through his one-night celebrity stands—with girl research students auditing conferences, angling for scarce jobs. Still, he needed the security of knowing he was continuously good, back home—an illusion that he wouldn't wish to be shattered by obvious good acting on Ruth's part. Yet since Ruth was supposed to be some kind of actress, he could watch out for signs of acting, and when he didn't find them—she not being good enough to produce them—that proved he was the active, sexy, stimulating one.

But what role did Richard think he was playing himself? Conducting this unsatisfactory, diffident, basically nonproductive affair with Ruth? (For they had only, in truth, been to bed twice.) Maybe he needed the security of her evasiveness as surely as Paul needed the prop of her deficiencies. (He wouldn't use a harder word.)

Evasions, deceits . . . What did they matter, after all? Paul had made the breakthrough here in Mezapico. That was real enough. The Footsteps of God would soon echo round the world.

As the Sierra slid down a one-in-four gradient of loose stones, Baby Alice protested at Ruth's overtight grip on her. A tiny simulacrum of Paul Hammond, she grunted and arched her back and flapped her hands. Then she squealed—repeating the pitched whistle of that Indian lad back in Ciudad Juarez.

"Why couldn't you leave Ally with Consuela? You know this road's lousy—"

"Leave Ally?" Ruth inquired in all innocence. "But I wanted her to see the whales."

"You must be joking," guffawed Paul. "At five months old, she'd never know if one leaped right out of the sea in front of her? Besides, we'll be hundreds of feet up a cliff, I gather from Richard."

"It's something to tell her when she grows up."

"Tell her anyway. She'd never know the difference."

"That's not honest, Paul. I'm a poor liar. . . ."

"As we're all being so honest today," Richard blurted, bitter at the discordant notes increasingly contaminating the whale migration for him, "that kid back there wasn't wolf-whistling anybody, Ruthy."

It was regretted as soon as said; for Ruth shot back angrily, "How would *you* know?"

"There's a whistle code," he mumbled, hurt by the scorn implied in the "you." "You find whistle codes in Turkey and the Pyrenees and here in Mexico. You saw them whistling at the Big Dish as we left, using it as a reflector?"

"I thought they were just having fun, making echoes," she muttered, crestfallen, as Paul slewed round another bend to bring them in view of San Pedro de la Paz, last and largest of the towns on their road seaward. San Pedro sprawled a thousand feet below them on the coastal plain: tiled white houses and glittering tin shanties dominated by a Spanish Colonial church of some Baroque magnificence, if rather sugary in execution. The town spread out around a baseball-diamond-size *zocalo* before the church like a crowd of diffident paupers invited to a wedding reception at which there was only one course: the huge three-tiered wedding cake.

"No, it's a way of signaling long-distance, Ruthy," he explained, trying to sound merely informative. "Can't blame them with all these hills! That's how they knew about the whales being on the move, all the way up there on the mountain."

He demonstrated, pushing his finger in his mouth the way the boy had.

"You don't use the vocal cords, just the tongue. Shove it into the right shape with your finger; then your larynx acts as a piston. Whistles carry five or six miles on a still day. That kid was probably warning folks: get out of the way, a car's coming. . . ."

"What do you know? Nice idea while it lasted—"

"You'd be surprised how similar these whistles and whale whistles look on oscilloscope photos!" he enthused earnestly. "Maybe the Mezapico could whistle to the whales if they put their minds to it." He laughed, awkwardly.

"Richard's so well up on whales, Ruth," grinned

Paul. "He'd be running 'em through mazes for a hobby. If they weren't so darned big. . . ."

"Have the Indians got something religious about whales, then? Some myth, if they're whistling about them?"

Richard shook his head.

"No, they're just hoping one of the grays will blunder ashore, for its meat. Sometimes one gets marooned."

"Why, what a feast!" She brightened—suddenly becoming gay and generous. "Why not whistle them ashore, to feed the Indians? Like the sirens whistled Ulysses! There's so much hunger in the world. . . . Look at Africa. It'll be as bad here soon. And Uncle Sam's granary's empty for handouts nowadays."

"You mean, imitate the distress call?"

"Is there one? You know it?"

"Sure he does," said Paul. "Richard listens to whale music like other folk listen to Bacharach."

"A one-time banquet wouldn't alter anything, Ruthy—only wipe out some whales. That's no answer. You have to do something fundamental about the agriculture. Anyway, the climate's stable here— it's not like Africa. It's always been the same as this."

She gestured mockingly at the stony terraces of scrub marching down toward a rocky desert plain.

"So the Indians are supposed to groove on these rocks and dust? I wouldn't mind a feast myself, in this place!"

Richard shook his head unhappily.

"So many humans, too few whales. It's unfair. They're remarkable creatures. We probably don't realize just how remarkable, because their world's so alien to ours. Some of them might be as intelligent as we are—"

Ruth leaned over the baby.

"D'you hear, Ally," she whispered into the softly pulsing fontanelle—as though information was more easily conveyed to the baby's brain by that route, "we're going to see some genius whales. Like your Pa, only bigger."

"Actually, it's the toothed whales that could be the clever ones. The sperm whales. The killers. Not the grays. They're just grazers, and probably a bit dim."

"Correction, Ally, we're going to see some stupid whales."

"I didn't say that either!"

Impossible to be sure of anything with Ruth. He was beginning to loathe her deviousness. He concentrated on the idea of the whales as something wholesome, with integrity.

Meanwhile Alice gyrated her hands, grunted like a little cream pig, and flexed her spine in a series of violent jerks.

And Paul Hammond chuckled.

"Let's get down to business, Richard. How to organize Max."

Five

Ten-Arms discharges a fluid blob that disperses into a cloud of echoes, making the creature seem more daunting still. Arms are haloed in sleeves of illusion as they wave and flex. Inside that cloud waits steel strength, hard beak, a thousand ripping suckers.

It's self-conscious, too, in its own indefinite enigmatic way, this tough gelatinous lurker. A potent awareness. Its tiny ten-arm cousins of the surface are toys to it, squirting their way about in clouds of themselves, a dozen a mouthful—slithery mulch drink. The great Ten-Arms thinks cold, dark thoughts down here, transforming them into light patterns bright enough for his own kind's bowl-eyes to read, printed out on blackness. Perhaps the Old Ones in the Star of Thought know something of Ten-Arms' ideas and what their lights say. Just now, its lights are only transient arbitrary mosaics upon the surface of a sullen, ravening identity.

Ten-Arms can feed him half a day. Fought and subdued, it rips into delicious chunk bites. Its arms, robbed of their suction, slide down his throat to plump his belly. His feces taste of the beast as they squeeze into the sea, later on. . . . Already he savors it down to those last fecal traces.

But he doesn't attack.

Eight-Arms is nesting in his head . . .

Ten-Arms flails a long thin tentacle, terminating in a broad fat swingle tip, toward him. Its other thicker arms splay out, sucker pads agape. And it pulses lights at him, buried in its flesh. Soft rose and blue jewels light up below its eyes. An emerald bulb blazes where the swingle flail joins the main tentacle strand. Tiny nacreous portholes line its body. Sapphires sit beneath its tail flaps. A shifting harlequin cloak of lights glows through the thinning fog, pulsating on and off.

Saying something? Luring?

Truth is, he barely sees these lights at all, only a faint, peripheral glow.

Long boneless fingers branch from around a mouth. A great flexing *hand* hangs there before him (carved in his melon,) lopped off above the wrist so that flaps of flesh splay loose behind. Inset in the palm is a beaked mouth. Those staring dome-eyes replace the knuckles. Obscene, disembodied hand, floating in void, groping at him. . . . Horror ghost of a hand!

The faint teasings of an itch begin to rasp his neck. Eight-Arms is restless. Its suckers need number-clicks to play with from the air . . .

So he must swing skyward on the long corkscrew climb sheer up canyon cliffs, empty-mouthed. As he surges, the beast flicks a thong at him that grazes his hide and sucks tight for a second, then tears free as his momentum carries him up. He catches a brief parting glimpse of its winking lights, from one eye. On and off—pink, silver, blue. Sees them in monochrome, hazy meaningless dots . . .

Surfacing, he snorts oily foam from his nostril, acrid with the poisons dissolved in it. Blows, and blows again; and wallows, gasping in fresh air.

The itch grows harsher, till he humps himself high in the waves, and a click-train echoes in his head from nowhere. Eight-Arms in his mind faithfully records it, to tell him what it means. Ducking below the surface then, ravenously, he searches for a school of albacore sweetmeats or a cloud of tiny ten-arms.

Curiously, that noise-burst in his head is associated with tenderness now; and though he fled from a steel fist, only to meet an open hand of horror in the depths, the ghost fingers that brush his consciousness now are tender.

Eight-Arms nesting at the back of his head is himself. An aspect . . . He accepts that, for the moment. It tells him things he needs to know. He tells it things to signal. They collaborate. He cannot count, as it can. Without being able to count, he couldn't signal. He counts upon it, yes! For a time, he feels quite euphoric.

But who is he signaling to, out there in the air?

The only way he can touch fingers, that once touched him—to which he owes a duty of love.

Leaving the mountain range behind him, he scans out across open sea till he catches up with a sweetmeat school and feasts on half a dozen members of it, tossing oily succulent meat back with his tongue. . . .

Once again, the spasm in his head has been witnessed. It puzzles the bull cruising by, whose melon overheard the faint fast train of clicks.

Six

The cliffs beyond San Pedro fell sheer to a narrow stony beach raked by foaming waves. In a few places they had eroded into scree slides like tailings from a mine, and precarious paths wound down these.

Several hundred yards offshore, the Californian grays swam by on the first leg of their four-and-a-half-thousand-mile migration from the warm Mexican breeding lagoons to the Arctic.

"They don't look gray to me," Ruth remarked in a hurt, cheated voice as she held Alice aloft pointlessly to see the view.

"Well, Richard?" laughed Dr. Paul. He seemed in an ebullient, generous mood now that he imagined he had successfully imposed his view of Max on Richard. Richard had promised to visit Max this evening to talk things over; however, now that he'd heard Paul out, Richard felt rather more sympathetic to Max Berg's viewpoint. Far back on Mezapico Mountain, the radio bowl caught and focused the sun: from this angle, with its gleaming superstructure, it seemed a table lamp plugged into the scenery,

28

switched on to lure giant moths. Did the priests in San Pedro ever worry in case it upstaged their glittering wedding cake in the popular imagination? Its sheer size and silence made it so ambiguous an artifact. If Dr. Paul had his way—the Christian Barnard of Radio Astronomy, performing a "soul transplant" of God into Science—religion and technology would soon enough to bedfellows. And a second Nobel prize for the discoverer of Hammond Waves would be just a reach away. . . .

Richard lifted his binoculars to watch the whales.

"The gray bits are just patches of barnacles," he explained. "The skin's black, basically. But most whales are misnamed, anyway. Killer whales aren't psychotic murderers. They can be as tame and friendly as you like. The sperm whale hasn't got gallons of sperm in that great head of its—the early whalers just called it sperm. Nobody really knows what the stuff's for even now—"

Dozens of mottled black backs ploughed northward through blue waves, presenting smooth, gently humped profiles as they cut the water, blowing low spouts like garden sprinklers switching on and off. Rose trees, woven temporarily out of spray: a fluid garden sprouting from the Pacific.

"Why *are* you so keen on whales?" Ruth asked him, nodding at the ocean, and those dark spouting shapes cleaving it so purposefully. "I mean, you're an astronomer. What's the connection?"

Dr. Paul chuckled.

"The connection, my dear, is the concept of intelligent life in the universe. There was a very wasteful, diversionary conference at Princeton a while ago about methods of eavesdropping on supposed advanced civilizations out in space. What a frivolity! Fortunately the dolphin buffs were there, arguing that we already have our own homegrown aliens here on Earth—these whales and whatnot—and we can't even communicate with them yet. . . . Which neatly shot down the proposal for an international listening project. That wasn't their intention, of course. But that was the upshot." Paul cracked his knuckles, smugly. "Personally, I don't give a damn about dolphins. Or nearby stars. Or anything that happened in the past billion years. In my book, the only knowledge worth knowing is way out there at the beginning of time—or the edge of space, whichever you prefer —in the background radiation supposedly left over from the fireball. Eh, Richard?"

Damn you, Paul Hammond, smarted Richard. In the midst of soliciting my support, you still find time to pour scorn on my "hobby"—my "eccentric amusement" . . .

"Paul's always hankered after finding the original *Fiat Lux* written out somewhere in the sky—scientifically," he said sarcastically to Ruth. " 'Let There Be Light.' So now he's found it. And to think, if I hadn't been at that conference, I wouldn't be here now, and part of it! No wonder I love whales and feel protective—they brought us all together. . . ."

"That's where I hired Richard, right," nodded Paul, ignoring whales and ocean—staring steadfastly inland toward his telecope. "Richard performed some rather elegant Ph.D. work—radio map of part of the Milky Way in the infrared. Good apprentice stuff. Nice sense of chutzpah, too. A thesis exactly one page long! Admittedly the page measured six feet by three feet and took two years to do. Still, it must be great telling people who've written whole volumes that you got your doctorate for a one-page thesis—I envy you, Richard. . . ."

"I still don't get why you were there, Rich," grumbled Ruth.

Richard smiled thinly.

"I published a piece about the radio clicks we hear from the stars, and the clicks the sperm whales make. Both, considered as pure mathematical information. I suggested at the conference maybe we could invent a cosmic syntax out of whale-talk, to speak to the stars—if we ever located anything, anywhere, to talk to."

"Now, that was naughty of you," reproved Hammond. "Fortunately, nobody pays any attention to the *Worm Runners Digest*. It's just a spoof journal— *Mad* magazine for scientists."

"It contains spoofs. But serious stuff, too. That's why it has two titles, the other one being *Journal of Biological Psychology*, remember?"

"To be sure, to be sure . . ." conceded Paul, wandering off impatiently, as Baby Alice started up a grunting wheeze that rapidly climaxed in shrill cries of hunger. He hunkered down twenty yards away and began figuring on the back of an envelope.

"Damn it, it *was* a serious piece!" Richard shouted after him. "It just happens to be the sort of adventurous serious piece you have to present as a spoof, or you've got no reputation left. Unless your name's Hammond, of course!"

Dr. Paul looked up and nodded in full agreement. Richard's interest in whales was precisely the professional flaw that made him an acceptable colleague, in Paul's eyes: perfectly competent as a radio astronomer, but with this deviant skeleton in his mental cupboard.

"Didn't we bring some beer?" he called out.

"It's in back, in the Koolpak," muttered Ruth. "Will you oblige, Rich? While I see to Ally—"

Richard tugged the rear door open and stripped three cans of Nochebuena from the six-pack in the refrigerated box. Propping the cans on the engine hood, he ripped the tabs off and flicked them away among the stones where they glinted like tinfoil flowers. The cans were already slippery with mist from the sudden change of temperature. He handed one to Ruth who was sitting in shade with her back up against the front wheel. She held Alice splayed on her knees—the baby alternately gobbling milk from a disposable bottle and jerking her head aside, grunting and rejecting it.

The second can he carried over to Dr. Paul and stuck into his field of vision, midway between his face and the envelope, so as to avoid having to stoop or else stand by like a waiter.

The envelope, he saw, had the letters "MB," no doubt for Max Berg, ringed at the center, surrounded by mathematical doodles which obviously had some private code significance for Paul. "RK," he noticed —Richard Kimble?—was off somewhere at the edge of the envelope, enclosed within brackets shaped suspiciously like a large fish, or whale . . .

Paul Hammond was figuring out his algebra of people, and how to organize them.

He seemed unperturbed by Richard's scrutiny— as though some law of nature prevented Richard from understanding the mathematics of his own manipulation. Accepting the beer, Paul set it down, then fiercely slit the envelope open with one finger and flattened it out. The name Hammond, contained in the address, abruptly entered the world of his calculations then, as *deus ex machina*, bulking large. Paul drew a long line out to it and circled it with an ellipse—an elliptical galaxy, no less—and grinned quickly and complacently up at Richard, as though to show he had been three steps ahead of his thoughts all the time. Defeated, Richard withdrew.

The baby's bottle lay duly disposed of on the ground—to end up in some shanty by nightfall, be used and reused by some enterprising Indian mother, till her child died of enteritis. . . . Stooping, Richard picked the plastic bottle up and squeezed it between his palms till it cracked open, before tossing it far away.

"It isn't like handing on used clothes," he explained gently to Ruth. But all she said was:

"Someone's snooping on us, Rich."

Sure enough, a hundred yards further along the cliff-top beyond Paul, unnoticed till now, an Indian squatted motionless in a dingy serape and straw hat, blending him in perfectly with the scenery. Indeed, he *was* scenery, compared with Dr. Paul.

"So watch him back," he laughed, pushing the binoculars toward her.

"But what's he *doing?*" she insisted, a note of panic in her voice. She clutched the binoculars briefly, her fingers an apprehensive starfish that suckered tight then detached themselves, unwilling to use such an instrument—she must hate all breeds of the genus telescope by now.

"Same as us, I guess. Whale viewing." Richard surveyed the Indian through the glasses. An old fellow with the collapsing, varnished features of a mummy—basted by years in a slow oven.

"No strength for work anymore, so they sent him out here in case a gray gets stranded—"

"Rich, let's tell him the distress call?" she begged suddenly. "Give him the jackpot!"

"No, I told you. Anyway, it's on tape in my room, not in my head. . . ."

Fortunately Alice began fretting again. They had to take turns pretend-walking her along an inch above the ground, to appease her. Richard was able to slip off Ruth's hook.

The baby's legs kicked woodenly in a puppet parody of tasks they'd be able to accomplish only many months later. Yet Alice was already sensing the freedoms of the future, as teasing ghosts producing a mixture of joy and frustration.

"Must be hell being a baby," muttered Ruth, sympathetically. "Locked up in this thing is a human being wanting to be let out." Subsiding on the ground by the cliff edge, she perched Alice on her knee.

"Hello sea, hello whales," she sang.

Alice stared down at her own hands, pouching her cheeks large in the process; then began slapping her fists about violently, striking rubbery blows at her mother and herself.

"How stupid *are* babies, Rich? I mean, biologically. Lord, it's sickening—"

"It isn't stupidity, Ruthy. Her brain's like a house in the process of being built. Where does she live till it's built? That's the hell of it. She's got to live in it—but most of it's still in the blueprint stage on the drawing board. So she's got to inhabit a mental plan—a sort of intuition of the house-to-be. She can sense what's coming, but she can't make use of what she's still making. It must be hellishly frustrating. No wonder babies cry."

He slumped with his back to the pitted chrome bumper, accepting the baby from Ruth and gazing into Alice's eyes, wondering what the baby's mind made of his image reflected in them.

The miniature face with tousled black hair and knotty woolen eyebrows thrusting out over rimless tinted spectacles—effectively rimming the lenses, furry caterpillars roosting on them. The snub nose, constantly wrinkling the glasses back up itself toward the knotty fuzz—a quizzical, rabbity habit ingrained in him by now.

Outside the clear mirror of the pupil, the iris imposed a blue filter; finally, the nacre of the cornea sheathed his features behind mother-of-pearl glaze. The reflection gradients were enchanting.

"I keep on wondering," he remarked to Ruth, "what other sorts of houses could be built from the same material. Trouble is, it's only when we've built our house that we can really use it to look out of the windows at the world. And the placement of windows dictates the view. That's really why I like thinking about the whales. The possibility of other houses, other views. Not that nonsense I said earlier."

Ruth had squirmed back against the bumper beside him. Seeing her thus in conjunction with the car, in classic ad-mag style, he felt that maybe whales were more reliable than people as an emotional focus. For him, at any rate. The whale was a fine symbol of the emotionally spontaneous, communicative existence. . . .

Basically, Paul's bleak new cosmology appealed to the resigned streak in him, he decided.

Finally, Hammond ambled over, satisfied with his calculations, and they finished the other three cans of Nochebuena beer.

As they left, the old Indian stuck a finger in his mouth and whistled.

"Whale come ashore?" Ruth said hopefully.

"Doubt it," shrugged Richard. "Us leaving, more like. Road safety. They like to keep tabs on us."

He talked some more about whales and whistle codes, then, still vainly trying to upgrade his preoccupation in Paul's eyes.

"Whistling's also a magical ritual for encouraging the maize to grow, did you know? The Mezapico believe humans used to be able to talk to plants in whistle speech. Gods and spirits used whistle speech too, to talk to sacred plants like the peyotl cactus. And to the stars in the sky! If the Indians only knew we were listening to clicks and whistles from beyond the stars! If they only knew how whales whistle to each other in the sea!"

They passed through San Pedro in a flurry of dust and started climbing steeply—Ruth clutching hold of Alice while Paul wrenched the Sierra round the bends.

"Whales whistling at the stars!" Paul laughed heartily, deliberately mixing up what Richard said. "If they could only hear the Footsteps of God, as we have. Now, that might be something."

"Those bangs and whimpers," recalled Ruth, as though it was something trivial that had slipped her mind.

"We've been analyzing all the whimpers following on the Big Bang, Ruth. The original fireball must have been ten billion degrees—it's cooled now to three degrees absolute, everywhere we look in the sky...."

"Uh? Everywhere? It must have been in one direction or another, your starter's pistol."

"No, no," Paul snorted, hardly realizing he was being goaded. "All space and time as we know them are products of the fireball. So we're still *inside* it. Only, it's vastly spread out by now and congealed into stars and galaxies, which we're part of, don't you see? Yet for this very reason it oughtn't to be possible to talk in terms of 'inside' or 'outside' the fireball. Of a shell, if you like, which we're inside of, and something else outside. Right?"

"Shells need a mommy hen, to lay them," she smiled sweetly, as they scattered the chickens of Ciudad Juarez.

"We've detected discrepancies in the background radiation. They're like little pinpricks we can listen through. Only, they're so far off they're really huge rips in the fabric of our reality. I guess you could call them windows on—"

"God tiptoeing round the heavens like a great big hen leaving claw marks in it . . . it's hilarious," she giggled, a heckler in the heart of his audience.

"Yes, damn it, *God!*" he snarled. "Out there—on the outside."

Ruth must have been holding Alice painfully tight. The baby cried aloud and her face suffused with blood. Her head became a beetroot registering infinite, however temporary, grief.

As they passed through Mezapico itself, the same priest was still standing in his church doorway, a thin black silent figure. He couldn't have been standing there all this time gazing up glumly at the telescope, thought Richard. It was a coincidence.

Seven

"A six-year-old defector, did you say? *Six?*"

Orville Parr swiveled his chair around and stared out at the cityscape of Tokyo. Beyond the few sad gray pines grouped around the embassy annex was one stream of traffic on ground level and a second stream flowing along above the first one on the overhead expressway which straddled the under-street on massive squat legs. Both streams were dense with delivery trucks and neon-striped taxis weaving between them with crazy bobsled bursts of speed. Taxis bright as butterflies: streaked with dayglo yellow, red, and orange. Almost as erratic as butterflies too!

Japan's a neon-painted taxi, reflected Parr. A metal butterfly chasing the pollen of a fare twenty-four hours a day. Without pollen it sickens and dies. Without honey it starves. So ever more frantically it flutters in desperation as it senses the long winter approaching. . . .

Red and white checked balloons hung out in the gray haze—beach balls bobbing on the smog surf. The neon ads that usually ran up and down their long tethers night and day, processions of Japanese characters streaming into the sky and back again, had been switched off; the absence of these bright streamers, and eclipse of the great roof signs, had a depressing effect on him. Gray pulluted days craved their gaiety. A specter of abandoned beaches—sadness of childhood winters around Cape Cod—overwhelmed him. Those balloons—drifting blindly on a sea of gas—were paraphernalia left outside locked chalets at the end of a season, for winter storms to wash away . . . Sad.

"He's called Nilin," offered Gerry Mercer, as though Parr ought to know the name. Was this child, found adrift in a fishing boat off Hokkaido, the northern island, supposed to be the son of somebody important? That didn't make him a defector. Perhaps the surly, moronic attendant accompanying him was the real defector. Perhaps he'd kidnapped the kid to pay for his passage to the States?

Obviously the boy would have to be handed back.

Orville Parr was rotund and balding, with a pasty complexion. His face sagged, a mass of unbaked dough in which features had been roughly punched —they slid downhill under the tug of gravity, and a small gritty moustache failed to stem the rout of flesh toward a bulging neck.

Gerry Mercer exemplified the archetypal agency blunder for a "cultural secretary": crew-cut athlete dressed in a severe charcoal suit with lapels thin as shoelaces, bright vulgar blue tie knotted impeccably tight. The knot—tiny head of a sapphire viper— nudged against his prominent Adam's apple, about to bury fangs in it. His voice bobbed eagerly:

"We already flew them down from Wakkanai. They're at Tachi now. The Japanese are amenable— so long as they have access and a casting vote. But dammit, Orville, the kid's asking for asylum with *us*, not the Japanese."

Parr made a gesture of disgust.

"How can he be? What a mess. So you've pushed all the panic buttons on account of some halfwit hijacking a kid. Why not leave them in Hokkaido? Let the Japanese handle it?"

"But it's Nilin," insisted Gerry. "At least it *seems* to be—"

Parr's attention was distracted by a mini-truck scooting along the overhead road in a blue fume cloud. Garish wreaths of plastic flowers on tripods three meters high bestrode it: plastic conservatory on wheels, hurrying to the opening of some pinball parlor or demise of some company chief. Hugely swollen, lavishly bright flowers—the appropriate blooms for a poison gas environment. Any flowers had to be overbright to compensate for the poor visibility; their plastic had been spun out of the same petrochemicals that hung combusted in the atmosphere. . . .

On the roof of a high-rise, of the same dusty color as chewing gum, a huge Nikon camera loomed—broad as the building it rested on. Generally the giant model rotated on a turntable. It had been switched off, too. Its lens pointed monotonously in their direction now, as though keeping the American embassy under surveillance.

Tokyo's red and white striped version of the Eiffel Tower pushed up its absurdly thin etiolated spike beyond, lit by a red aircraft warning beacon: a solitary candle left burning in the sky. He could just barely trace its thin candy limbs in the smog from this marker downwards.

They were having to burn low-grade high-sulfur fuel oil in the factories mostly, these days, or else close them down.

"Surely you mean Nilin's son?" A faint light dawned. A Soviet cosmonaut who'd vanished some years before, presumed killed in a launch pad explosion at Tyuratam. He'd been called Nilin, hadn't he? But what use would the six-year-old son of a dead cosmonaut be, except to harm Soviet-American relations? Was some plot brewing in the inner circles of the agency, that Gerry was privy to, and not Parr? But the logic broke down. A boy adrift with a dimwit in the waters between Sakhalin and Hokkaido . . . no one could possibly attach any importance to it, except as a routine case of air-sea rescue. Probably the boy's mother worked on Sakhalin now, in one of the Far East Center research stations . . .

"Nilin never married," Gerry said briskly, as though reading Parr's thoughts. "He had no kids. It's Nilin himself, I think."

"What do you mean? It's nonsense. Nilin was this cosmonaut who got killed at Tyuratam, right? Or is there some other Nilin?"

"It's the same one. Georgi Knipovitch Nilin. Only presumed killed, Orville. He just never appeared in any more cosmonaut group photos after the accident. No specific announcement about him, though."

"Is there ever? So this *boy* is the same Nilin? You must have taken up reincarnation, Gerry! Say, why don't you apply for an assignment with the Dalai Lama? Then if he dies you can liberate Tibet single-handed in search of his new body. Mystical espionage —how's that grab you?"

As Parr swung his chair around again to survey Gerry irritably, the Adam's apple hobbled up and down in embarrassment—or discreet fury.

"Okay, Orville, I admit the boy's in a confused state. He acts schizophrenic part of the time, and plain autistic the rest, not communicating at all, just making bits of nonsense apparatus out of any scraps of wire or screws or light bulbs he can find lying around. But during the communicative phases he comes out of himself enough to put something across —even if it is like a pair of Siamese twins fighting over who gets to speak. He's said these incredible things—in broken English, as well as Russian. That he's Nilin. That he's a spaceman—"

"Any kid's fantasy. If he's autistic, he wants to escape. Where better than into a space capsule? Presumably he's been kidnapped from a mental hospital by one of the attendants. What has the attendant got to say about it? He stole the boat—"

"He doesn't know much except he loves the boy like any dumb stalwart in a Russian novel. He's a great strapping *muzhik* of a peasant. He carries the boy round like some little prince he's protecting—"

"Perhaps it's a great-grandson on the Romanovs?" Parr inquired sarcastically. "So the man says the boy wants to go to America—meaning that he does himself? It's so obvious."

"No—the *boy* says he wants to go there! We've interrogated him in Russian and English. He's *defecting* to us; he knows the English word. He says he has Nilin's mind. It's a terrible effort for him framing sentences, getting his thoughts straight. A few rocks are pushing up, but the tide keeps on washing back over them. He gave details to the base commander at Wakkanai that a kid just couldn't know—about the Soviet space program. About rocket engines. Six years out of date, of course—and only fragments—and it exhausted him so much he went into withdrawal again—but it was totally convincing."

"The attendant could be a KGB agent for all you know. Told the boy what to say. We could be walking into a trap. Though why it's being set eludes me."

"It smells real, Orville. You don't get a six-year-old behaving the way Nilin does."

"The pseudo-Nilin . . . Well, what's the explanation?"

"The attendant said someone was printing babies' minds. He used the word 'printing,' same as you print a book or print currency. But he doesn't know how to explain properly. He's a dumb hick."

"With a heart of gold. I'll believe it when I see it," Parr groaned.

What do you do to normalize a mentally deranged six-year-old? Take him to the zoo for a treat, suggested Bob Pasko, the base psychiatrist at Tachikawa —a hairy man with a head as curly as a black lambs-wool beret, a perpetual five o'clock shadow and stray curls even pushing their way through his shirt front by way of the buttonholes. Let him see other kids behaving naturally, enjoying themselves. His own self might emerge from the fog it's in.

The three days that had passed since the boy's arrival saw little real clarification of the dilemma he posed; but enough hints to exonerate Gerry Mercer, to Parr's annoyance. Parr still felt suspicious of the pseudo-Nilin, as he insisted on calling him, as a novel gambit in the intelligence game. If this was the case, however, it was far from clear why he had been planted—hints of experiments in brainwashing babies could hardly redound to the Russians' credit.

Pasko had seen many damaged minds during a service career stretching back to the early days of the Vietnam buildup. He surmised that the child showed all the signs of a major psychological trauma brought on by some prolonged effort using hallucinogens, to persuade him that he was someone other than who he was. Not a boy of six, but an adult named Georgi Nilin. His periods of communicativeness were dominated by the false information he'd been fed—misunderstood and served up in a garbled version. His periods of withdrawal, when he created strange "machines" out of whatever was at hand, constituted a typical autistic defence mechanism, in Pasko's diagnosis. The boy had been treated like a machine, so he surrounded himself with pseudo-machines to achieve a robotic salvation.

Physically, the boy's skull showed no signs of recent surgery—though it carried traces suggesting he'd been through operations shortly after birth, followed by stereotaxic probing, possibly lasting as late as his third year.

But what was the reason for it all? A sincerely meant, if brutal—and reprehensible—new therapy? That he came to be in their custody now, by this reading, was all the fault of the attendant Mikhail, who had plainly misunderstood everything he witnessed at the hospital on Sakhalin.

Yet the boy certainly asked for asylum during his communicative moments—plaintively and obsessively, in a reedy voice. . . . A plea for the security of the hospital he must have come from? But no, he begged in broken English—not a mental asylum, *political.*

"I am *failure,*" the boy proclaimed with absurd solemnity, struggling to master the shapes of the English sounds.

So to cheer him up, Pasko, Parr, and Mercer drove him and the inseparable Mikhail from the airbase to Tama Zoo nearby; taking along the embassy's naval attaché Tom Winterburn as Russian interpreter.

Already, by ten in the morning, schoolchildren crowded the wooden acres of the zoo. Sturdy little fellows in yellow plastic road-safety bonnets pursuing their flag-bearing teachers in dense streams. The children gazed at Georgi Nilin and the Americans and the great loutish Russian with such nonstop cheeky curiosity that Parr could only wonder whether Pasko was out of his mind, bringing the boy here. Was this his version of shock treatment? Total immersion therapy? In at the deep end!

"Haro, haro!" one after another of the seemingly endless stream of Japanese kids called out. And if you bumped into them! Kids they might be to look at— but they must be built of some sort of superflesh weighing heavier than American flesh. Mobile tree stumps marching along on their roots: knock into one, and it instantly locked to the ground. And so many of them, such a lopped-off forest on the move!

Definitely a mistake to come here. Parr glanced at the Russian child, being led along by his gangly *muzhik* attired in the same long flapping coat and felt boots as he'd arrived in, wondering if the boy felt the same panic as he did. At least Mikhail was making good headway through the flood of foreign children, keeping Nilin sheltered safe in the lee of his body as he paced evenly along.

But what a thin sallow slip of a lad, with his close-cropped spiky fair hair, among all these Japanese supertots! Nilin's features had a faintly Mongolian cast to them. Occasional flurries of effort passed over a bland blankness, like pond ripples. To Japanese eyes, the combination of fair hair and faintly Asiatic features must have made him seem a half-caste, no doubt accounting for the children's continuing amusement.

"Haro, Amerikajin!" they cried.

All the six- to nine-year-olds in the Greater Tokyo area must be here today. Parr felt he was stuck in some crowded elevator between floors.

This couldn't be real! Just round the corner some magician must be stamping all these kids out of rice-cake or reinforced paper, patting them on the head, setting them in motion. Yes—working overtime, too, with some heavy-gravity paper imported direct from Jupiter, that could knock a grown man off his feet!

Caught in an eddy between twin streams of the yellow bonnets, their group gravitated towards a cement hillside walled off by a deep dry moat, where brown bears were prowling.

A stink of pungent grease drifted toward them from the beasts. They smelt rancid, despite innumerable dunkings as they shoved each other underwater in a shallow pond on the hill with massive playful paw clouts. Maybe they were in heat? In the fall?

As the breeze veered, the stink diminished; but catching a whiff of people, the largest male reared up in turn, nose twitching and little gimlet eyes peering myopically at them.

"How do you like the bears, Georgi?" Pasko asked in a playful tone, Tom Winterburn translating dutifully. The naval attaché was a lofty, bony, watery-eyed individual with long sharp icicle features which always seemed faintly blue at the extremities, with too little blood to feed the skin stretched out so tightly across his frame. He was perpetually sucking his cheeks in, collapsing and pursuing them—transforming his already gaunt head into the deflated rubber lung of an anesthetizer.

The boy stuttered:

"*Gdyeh del'finy?*"

"Is there a dolphinarium? He wants dolphins."

"Gerry, you kept the tickets. There's a plan of the zoo on the backs."

Mercer consulted the rear of the long blue tickets hopelessly. The locations were all printed in Japanese.

"I can't remember the character for dolphin," he admitted finally—if he had ever known it.

"Here, give them over," Parr said. "Dolphinarium won't be written in characters. It's a foreign word, so it'll be in the kana script."

He hunted round the maze printed on the ticket, before triumphantly stabbing his finger at a short line of jagged simple shapes, like cuneiform.

"Do-ru-fi-na-ri-u-n," he pronounced slowly. "That's it. And we're beside the bears. Bear is *kuma*, but . . ." He remembered a restaurant in the Shinjuku amusement area selling, or purporting to sell, roast bear-meat, with the character for *kuma* carved over the door; but the character swam in his mind's eye indistinctly, changing shape all the time. He shrugged. "What's next along here? Elephants . . . They'll have to be written in kana. . . . Yes, here we are. So we need to go on past the elephants, then turn right."

Those elephants definitely were in heat. A black rubber cosh hung down behind the bull's hind legs, two feet long. It stiffened as he nuzzled the cow with his trunk, though he didn't seem to have the energy to do much more with his magnificent member than engorge it softly. They probably only fed them buckets of vitaminized rice, Parr thought. Inadequate diet. Who could afford to feed an elephant these days?

When they reached the dolphinarium, it consisted of an outdoor pool and a large gray building adjacent. A submarine channel connected them. Two dolphins were circling listlessly in the pool outside, beneath a hoop on a pole intended for them to leap through. Dozens of yellow bonnets crowded the parapet round the pool, calling for the dolphins to perform and throwing candy through the hoop, which the dolphins ignored as it hit the water and sank.

Nilin tugged violently away from the pool toward

the gray building, crying, "V*nutri, vnutri!*" in his thin voice.

"He wants to see inside."

Indoors, the dolphinarium was a grim dismal hall with a long plate-glass window giving an underwater view of a large, deserted tank. The only enlivening feature of the tomblike place was a large mural depicting the family tree of the whales and dolphins with colored drawings and captions in Latin and Japanese.

Nilin forced himself up against this clammy mural on tiptoe, then sagged back and indicated urgently that Mikhail should lift him. The tall Russian picked him up, and the boy drew a circle around one particular picture in the condensation damp with his fist —setting drops of water scurrying towards the floor. He swung back explosively in Mikhail's grasp, twisted his face towards Pasko and shouted at him the one phrase:

"Jonah Kit!"

It was the sperm whale, Latin name *Physeter catodon,* that he'd circled.

"That's odd," remarked Winterburn. "The Russian word for whale is *kit.* But they don't call that particular one a *kit.* A sperm whale is *kachalot* in Russian . . ."

"That's the whale that swallowed Jonah?" Gerry asked brightly.

The child screamed a string of Russian words at them then, ending up by throwing his frail body at the mural, clawing it with his fingernails as if to burrow inside the picture. He would have hurt himself, if Mikhail hadn't gently detached him—and when Mikhail did so, moving a few feet away, the boy's face abruptly lost all expression. A switch was turned off. He went limp, catatonic.

"What did he say?" demanded Pasko.

"He said, the first printing is a baby. This is the second printing—"

"For God's sake! They're trying to brainwash kids into thinking they're animals? So that's the next stage after Nilin, is it? No wonder he defected . . ." The psychiatrist ran his hand through his curls. "But the 'Wolf-child' phenomenon is supposed to be just a popular myth to explain autistic reactions, damn it! Is this an even more radical treatment for deranged children they're working on?"

"If you take him literally," Parr pointed out, "you wouldn't produce wolf children. You'd produce whale children. I hardly see the sense in that. You might persuade a kid to scamper about on all fours barking at the moon, but this would be like telling him he's a bird and expecting him to fly!"

"What's special about a sperm whale, Tom?" Pasko asked thoughtfully.

"Dives deepest of any of the whales. Holds its breath the longest. I wonder . . . if this has got anything to do with autism at all? We've been training dolphins at San Diego for some time. But sperm whales? It's incredible. Yet the Russians aren't scientific idiots—unless they're off on another Lysenko track. . . . Now let me think. The Russians performed a complete about-face on whaling policy a couple of years back. Began grumbling that the sperm whale was an endangered species and needed strict protection. They're still happily slaughtering the other whales out of existence with their factory ships, but be damned if they didn't railroad this through the whaling commission. The Japanese hated it. Normally the Russians and Japanese ignore any kind of whale quotas. But we had to support the Russians on this, of course, because we'd started the conservation scare in the first place. . . ."

Schoolchildren chattered into the bleak hall, hooting echoes off the walls; then there were yellow bonnets everywhere—the luminous headgear reflecting the tank lights, a swarm of sulfurous jellyfish. Surging with panic, Parr bolted for the door.

Outside, he leaned against a wall, feeling his heart thump.

Oh for Cape Cod, deserted winter beaches and bracing air, a lifetime ago!

Something that had struck him as odd at the time fell into place now—or rather, didn't so much fall into place, as out of it. Mikhail had known exactly which whale the boy wanted to be held up to. Had held him directly in front of it. Yet the surly reticent peasant said nothing to them before about whales, only about children . . .

Eight

There would be no more casual outings to zoos. The Nilin affair had escalated to the level of an incident. When the meeting convened in Parr's office two days later, it was a far more serious affair.

"The Soviet embassy is aware that we have the boy," stated Captain Enozawa primly, stressing the word *we* faintly as reminder to the Americans of their status in Japan . . . a status constantly on the decline.

Once he'd been one of the bubble-gum-chewing crowd himself—on the morning when Japan's greatest novelist, Yukio Mishima, invaded the Self-Defense Force headquarters with his private bodyguard and tried to persuade the assembled soldiers to oust the Liberal Democrats and restore ancient values. He'd still been chewing gum derisively when Mishima slashed open his abdomen in ritual disgust and was beheaded by a friend. . . .

Enozawa had modified his values since then. Nowadays, as liaison officer for the Self-Defense Force, he was hovering on the verge of outright hatred of America. The mood shift only betrayed itself as yet by a purging of American slang and accent from his speech, however. And of gum from his mouth.

He wasn't alone. In a thousand unobtrusive shifts of emphasis up and down the Home Islands, the novelist's ritual suicide had registered, and was registering still—a slow earthquake, whose shock waves might take years to peak. . . .

Enozawa appeared superficially a neat and scrupulous officer, with a sophistical turn of mind, presumably due to his education at Tokyo's Jesuit-run Sophia University.

Quite wrong. This scrupulousness was an essential part of the new patriotism emerging in him. Patriotism had always been an aesthetic experience in Japan. Enozawa was pruning and cropping his spirit with all the subtle rigor of a bonsai gardener—all the neatness of a junior priest raking sand at the Ryoanji stone-garden temple. If these Americans could have seen the gum-chewing, Beatles-whistling cadet of a few years back. . . ! Jesuits be damned.

"The Soviet embassy attaches great importance to the boy. 'Request' is perhaps too delicate a term for their note requiring his return—along with boat and attendant. Do you suppose it is a coincidence that the fisheries conference has just been adjourned in Moscow? Remember the hardships we had in previous years. This has been used as a political lever before. Naturally it is a matter of priority to our government that the crab catch for the northern waters is finalized—"

"A hilarious hassle you had over those damn crabs last time," laughed Parr, in the belief that a little humor might help. "Your side arguing that the king crab leaps through the water and floats about like a Japanese paper fan. So it belongs to the open sea. Russians insisting it creeps along the sea bed, so it belongs to their own continental shelf as a Soviet citizen. Went on for six weeks, right "

"Resulting in a quota discrepancy in our disfavor of five thousand tons," Enozawa reproved. "We do not regard this as frivolous, Mr. Parr—in view of the riots in Tsukiji fish market. Russia is applying pressure on a sensitive nerve. The boy should perhaps be repatriated immediately—

"Incidentally," he added, "you refer to 'their' continental shelf. In the case of Kamchatka, yes. But Sakhalin and the Kurile Islands are quite another matter!"

"If they regard Nilin as so important," suggested Gerry, "we have to face the likelihood he's telling the truth. In which case, what the hell is going on on Sakhalin?"

"There's one strange thing I've discovered about their research station at Ozerskiy," began Tom Winterburn.

"At Nagahama," murmured Enozawa.

"Excuse me?"

"Nagahama is the correct Japanese name. Please remember, the whole Southern half of Sakhalin was simply confiscated from Japan in 1945—"

"Ozerskiy is what it says on the maps."

"Whose maps? Not Japanese maps, Captain Winterburn."

"Well, let's not create unnecessary confusions!" The naval attaché consulted the file before him, embarrassedly. "It seems the research center there has access to an American-made IBM 370–185 computer. I don't know if you appreciate the significance of this—"

"A pretty advanced machine for fisheries research," hazarded Mercer, the knot of his blue tie even tighter today—Enozawa watched this at least with tacit approval; but whether because it might garotte Mercer, or because it indicated a sharpening up of American sloppiness, was dubious. . . .

"Who's using what sort of hardware is a fair indicator of what's going on in the world. The Israelis have an Elliot 503 and an IBM 360–80 they use for hagiography—they worked out that three separate prophets wrote the Book of Isaiah—and an IBM 370–154 to handle air defense. The Burmese have one clapped-out ICL 1902 doing census work. The Japanese—" he nodded deferentially at Enozawa—"well, let's just say your homegrown computers and peripherals are competing very successfully on the U.S. home market. Now, our own old front runner, IBM's 370–165 series, can perform three million operations per second. But the best Soviet product, the BESM, can only handle five hundred thousand—*one-sixth* of that number. Admittedly export licenses are available for the Soviets to buy IBM 370–165s from us since the Kissinger commitment—so long as they only want them to organize soap factories and that kind of consumer job. But the real big baby—the 370–185—isn't to be had for love or money. *Yet,* they seem to have got hold of one by the back-door method. Through some dummy organization in Vienna. The 370–185 can carry out six million operations a second. But the Soviet 370–185 hasn't gone to the military—or the space program. It seems to have ended up in that little village of Ozerskiy on Sakhalin—"

"Nagahama," muttered Enozawa.

"Nagahama," nodded Winterburn, with a curt inclination of the head which might have been charitably taken for an abbreviated bow. "Information's scanty. Still, if the 370–185 job *is* there, and if this Nilin came from there and he's got anything whatever to do with it, he's not going straight back, dammit. Apologies to all your crab fishermen, but—"

"Gently," advised Parr, realizing how flat his own attempt at humor had fallen with Enozawa.

Winterburn bit his lip softly, pursed his cheeks.

"Your fishermen aren't being left out of this, Captain Enozawa. Obviously this concerns the whole Pacific basin. Resources, military—I can't say for certain." And the Japanese returned a smile faint and evasive as that on the face of a Noh mask.

"Getting back to whales," Pasko reminded, "put a sperm whale and an IBM 370–185 computer together, what do you get?"

"An electronic whale?" suggested Parr facetiously.

"A *programmed* whale," corrected Pasko. "But programmed with what? Nilin said he was a failure. The

first print was a human baby—namely himself. The
second print was—the whale. I'm just quoting him.
I've been wondering increasingly if those junk items
he puts together out of bits and scraps really do represent a standard autistic 'mechanical boy' reaction.
Maybe they're models of something he's seen, on Sakhalin. He hasn't the ability to describe verbally, or
even draw a picture, but he can show us something
obliquely—"

"We're all edging around the subject," Winterburn
said impatiently. "I see only two possible interpretations, in view of the 370–185. Either the Soviets have
developed a technique for programming sperm
whales to do what they want. Or—in view of Nilin
—some technique for printing the consciousness of
one human being onto another brain! Human adult
to human infant, initially. That explains Nilin. But
now they've gone on to human adult onto whale!"

"A response to your deep-submergence submarine
for the ULMS missiles?" suggested Enozawa quietly.

"This certainly puts their crusading at the whaling
commission in the proper perspective! The Soviets
jumped on that ecological bandwagon awful fast.
They haven't cared before—apart from a bit of piety
about Comrade Dolphin. The reason they gave for
not needing to catch sperm whales anymore was that
now they've found an alternative source for sperm
whale oil. Thousands of acres in Samarkand have
been turned out to jojoba cultivation in the past
couple of years. Jojoba's a Mexican weed—the oil
from its seeds is a perfect substitute for sperm whale
oil. The Soviets have gone into full production. They
imported tons of jojoba seeds from Mexico, and now
they're growing masses of it in Central Asia."

"How fortunate for them," commented Enozawa
acidly. "How unfortunate for us Japanese that we can
find no such substitute for the whale as a vital foodstuff—when Russians and Americans band together to
ban our fishing."

"This puts their decision in a new light, Captain
Enozawa. We were fooled. They've found a much

better use for the sperm whale—that involves not killing any of them, indeed making it illegal under international law. They plan to program the whales to control the seabed!"

"So that's that," sighed Parr. "We have no choice but to kick this thing upstairs, fast." He inspected Enozawa dubiously. "Can you possibly stall the Soviet embassy about Nilin—in view of all this?"

"Not *my* decision, Mr. Parr! That is not how we Japanese—"

"Yeah, I understand that—a consensus of decisions . . ."

Parr raised a hand to rub his neck. It had been developing a fierce itch lately whenever he sat by the window. He blamed it on the Nikon. The dummy camera was still pointing remorselessly at him over the rooftops.

Nine

He swims northward toward a Star of Thought being convened for him.

The Great Singing Ones passed news of it through the ocean waveguides, from a score of swimdays off, to the old bull who now watches him constantly while he forges north with his females about him. . . . The old bull passed the summons to him.

And the old bull tells him:

When Seven gather nose to nose and brow to brow in slack water, waving their flukes to stay in place, their seven melons of liquid wax cut off from the sea-world and look inward, not outward; become a closed system for their clicking thoughts. The pure ideas burst-pulsing in each other's melons echo, reecho, combine, and interfere . . . weave patterns larger than the pattern of an idea carved in oil-wax in any single brow. So the Glyphs of Awareness are born— which only a new Star-Gathering can fully open up again, which nonetheless linger on in the individual's memory in the meanwhile as foci.

For tens of thousands of sea-years Glyphs have been elaborating—passed on from Star to Star, down the swimming generations.

Our oil melon was much smaller once.

Did you guess that?

Now hugely enlarged, it lets us dive deep and hunt the Ten-Arms. It is both sound-screen and pressure-tank. But that is *by the way!*

In reality, we dived deeper and deeper for generations, to force our melons to grow large—and not the other way about!

For an eon Our Kind has been designing itself . . . so that we can come face to face with ourselves, carve out the Glyphs of Knowledge in oil-wax and click-songs . . .

Those Great Singing Ones? Who pass our click-songs on, a hundred or a thousand swimdays?

Don't understand them. Only sing them.

Criers across the sea-world, they have no Star themselves, no concept of a Star of Thought, no physical hope of this . . .

Can he give a new glyph of understanding to the Star? Young as he is, with his deviant talent for counting and sky-pulsing, he is *different*.

But sick maybe—in mind or melon? Warped in the womb by the faint traces diffusing through all oceans now . . . which His Kind taste with mounting apprehension such as no glyph has traced since that first Star was born on a cold flat ocean day a hundred thousand years ago—while ice was unlocking new mazes of the sea to north and south, and they tasted the planet changing . . .

Or is his alien pulsing the hint they need to read the light signals of the Great Ten-Arms in the deeps? That has only been a war of meeting-and-eating, till now. What mightn't those guess of the shape of reality, in their cold, violent, flexible way?

The Star calls him, to glyph out answers to certain enigmas . . .

Now, in addition to sky-pulsing a model of the sea and Steel locations, he feels bound—by a duty of love —to signal the fact of summoning to the Star.

He pulses, and dives compulsively, rising miles away and an hour later . . . to trek back to the herd.

Another night and a day, and questions come to him, which Eight-Arms in him wrestles into shape— awkward, itchy questions.

This Star of Thought? What is it? Describe. Explain.

He complies.

Then, the day after, the air says: Northward, find this Star! Which is as well, since he doesn't know how he could have disobeyed the itching peck in his neck —or the wailing summons of the Singing Ones—if the two were conflicting . . .

The air-clicks trigger another itch too. Sexual undercurrents swirl beneath his memory. Queer ghosts of "hands" upon his flesh, his flesh upon another's, turn him for comfort to a female of His Kind. He slides against her in the herd, though the musk tastes bitter, and all her signals are AVOIDANCE. He careens her with his body, shivering with excitement.

Irritably she slams her body against his; and through the waves come grating, angry pulses from the bull. . . .

Ten

A vulture perched on a lower spar of one of the limbs that swung the Big Dish around on its railway tracks. The bird regarded the garbage pit, where a muscular Indian youth was raking grit over discarded cans and bottles, with implacable beady patience.

The bird's posture wasn't so dissimilar from Dr. Paul's, thought Richard—sitting behind his desk there, betraying a certain tension by the set of his shoulders, yet in all other respects radiating the confidence of one about to flap his wings and descend on the carcass of the universe.

Richard, Paul, and Max Berg had been up all night correlating data from their partner Dish six thousand miles further south in the Andes that gave them their long baseline for detecting minute discrepancies in the radio sky.

Max Berg looked distinctly eroded by the experience—a quite unnecessary piece of scientific gymnastics, insisted on by Paul. He seemed waxy and diffuse now, melted down from his normal state of dynamic ampleness. His bones had given up weight-bearing some hours earlier. No doubt this was exactly what Paul had hoped for as an added bonus to getting the Footsteps material all neatly tied up. To the extent that Paul liked his *diktats* to be backed by some semblance of democracy, Max and Richard were two ponies harnessed to a racehorse in a troika of his own devising, the real function of which seemed to be to keep them simultaneously in check, and worked to their limits. Given the workload on the one hand, and the cooperative constraints of modern research on the other, colleagues were a sort of obligatory evil. Still, Paul Hammond kept his purely scientific staff to the minimum—though he splurged on the technical and operative side. There were a dozen electrical engineers, mechanics, and computer programmers at Mezapico.

Richard Kimble had his own strong suspicions by now as to why he himself had been hired.

Max Berg's case was similar, in some respects. The man was more stubborn and refractory than Richard, but deep down he too nursed a vulnerable broken-hearted core. Max had been released from Dachau on some obscure whim of irrational tyrants only days before the Second World War broke out and sailed for America only hours before he would have been trapped again. Paul could hardly do without his immense mathematical competence—yet he always knew that Max had been, in a sense, conditioned, like a maze-running worm, by shocks of physical and mental humiliation, and that something in him had snapped, and reknit only untidily. All that previous night Paul had been running him through the maze of figures for the greater glory of science cynically recreating the régime of the camp, it seemed to Richard. Max accepted the pressure for the sake of knowledge of the universe, perhaps hoping against hope that Paul would turn out to be wrong. Meanwhile the experience was subtly reconditioning him, recasting him in a previous, less ebullient psychic mold. The

fringes of his moustache looked thin and tatty in the
morning light, since he had kept himself awake
through the past twenty-four hours while he worked
only by pulling out the hairs one by one. He still nib-
bled at it every few minutes, stretching his upper
lip, tugging the hairs between his teeth, releasing
them.

Richard stared at the vulture, willing it not to
move. It wasn't likely to do so, while that Indian
stayed neat the trash pit; so this was a singularly
purposeless exercise of will. Perhaps he was really
willing Paul not to move—by a form of sympathetic
magic; not to flap his wings too wildly to attract the
world's attention. However, Paul Hammond was the
last one to be willed to avoid historic histrionics. . . .

"We're ready to make the announcement, right?"
Max sighed.

"This will put the cat among the pigeons, Paul. Is it
the right way to do it, I ask myself? Press agencies,
instead of the Seattle conference—?"

"The academic rigmarole in due course, Max. But
a breakthrough of this magnitude cries out for a far
more *generous* treatment!"

"It's vulgar, Paul. Not the scientific method."

"Sure, it's showbiz. Why pretend? Do you honestly
think we would be sitting here today, in Mezapico, if
I'd not been my own vulgar P.R. man?"

"Your other 'vulgarities' were minor ones compared
with what you're contemplating now. Wait till Seattle,
Paul. The news agencies will take it up soon enough.
But this haste, it's indecent! After a few billion years,
you can't wait a few more weeks! Paul, you're so
hooked on this catchphrase 'Footsteps of God' . . .
You know in your heart you don't dare entitle a *scientific* document that—"

"Oh, no?" laughed Paul brassily. "But I will! Didn't
they laugh at Hammond Waves, and wasn't I right all
along? Doesn't the world know it? A 'Topological
Catastrophe' invoking another galaxy colliding with
ours, but masked by the whole length of the Milky

The Jonah Kit 61

Way and the Lens Core—wasn't that a zany enough
sounding concept? And who was right? Tell me," he
clacked, eyes glinting, "do you challenge our present
conclusions? Are they invalid? No? Then it's our
bounden duty to broadcast them. People are dying
every hour without knowing the truth—it's disgusting.
Anyway, we're hardly doing Seattle a disservice. Au-
dience-wise, it'll be the first astrophysics conference in
history with standing room only."

What is paranoia? thought Richard. Delusion . . .
But there's no delusion involved in this. If Paul were
saying that the earth was square, it could be different.
And yet, it's something far more devastating he's pro-
claiming!

"Of course," Richard inserted, barbedly, "this might
—just *might*—spell the end of astronomy. Maybe we
should consider that aspect."

Paul stared through Richard at a point approximately two feet behind his head, as though he
couldn't believe that Richard Kimble had said those
particular words and was therefore trying to locate
the source of the voice.

Richard explained. "The funding for projects like
this is getting much tighter, right? You said so yourself. Announcing that you've finally reached the dawn
of creation, unlocked the last secret drawer, and
found it empty—presenting it in those explicit terms,
as you seem intent on doing!—well, most people are
bound to react to it as The Finale."

"Crap, Richard. On the contrary, it's bound to stim-
ulate a flurry of projects to confirm us or refute us. A
drought of funds? I'd look for a flood. The world will
be desperate to know one way or the other. The ultimate truth about the nature of matter—of reality! It
hasn't come from the particle accelerators. It's come
from us here."

Paul yawned harshly and abruptly.

"The end of astronomy?" he queried, archly. "As I
define it, 'end' means 'ultimate purpose' or 'ultimate
object.' Which is not piddling around with planets

and moons, but the study of ultimate origins, the basic
nature of things. Everything else that happened since
the Origin is inconsequential—"

"These modest statements of yours, Paul," sighed
Max, "how they endear you to us."

"These modest statements of mine will make you
famous, Max, and you, Richard, being my team—"

"—in whom you are well pleased," grimaced Max.
Dr. Paul only inclined his head in agreement, ob-
livious to the overtones, or acquiescing in them complacently.

"I shall contact the news agencies this evening.
Meanwhile, I've drafted a handout I want to read to
you. It isn't polished yet. But you'll be questioned
about this in a few days' time by uniformed journalists. So it would be a good idea if we mentally
drafted our own statements along these lines, to keep
everything crystal clear."

"Couldn't we go to sleep for a few days first?"
moaned Max. "It's like running a hundred miles, then
having to host a cocktail party."

"Cocktail party, Max? I call it the banquet of the
universe! Besides, it's been a quiet life here up until
now. We've had to keep quiet as mice," he chuckled,
"to hear those footsteps tiptoeing away . . ."

As. Dr. Paul lifted a sheet of typescript, the vulture
flapped off its perch and glided down toward the
vacated pit.

Paul's voice reminded Richard of the lime-flavored
candies he bought at a candystore as a child back in
Philadelphia—green crystal bullets of information
with fizzy, effervescent sherbet centers: Hammond's
best data packages . . .

"The farther out into the universe we look with our
radiotelescopes," rattled Hammond, "the farther back
we see into time itself toward the very start of the
universe. At eight to nine billion years ago, innumerable powerful radio sources indicate a caldron of activity. That is when the galaxies were first forming
—out of the energies we always supposed the primal
fireball to have liberated. Nine billion years ago,

there is only diffuse background radiation. Representing, supposedly, the cooling of the fireball itself—the heat echo of that initial act of creation. Now we have discovered, working at very low wavelengths in tandem with our Andes telescope, a number of discrepancies in this uniform microwave background . . ."

He paused briefly for breath, surveying his tired colleagues who in his eyes were now cutouts representing Reuters, UPI.

They're going to be furious in the Andes when Paul springs this, thought Richard. Has Paul even consulted them? But after all, isn't the Andes director in his pocket to a very substantial extent? An appointee of the junta—and the junta firmly in the pocket of Washington—and Dr. Paul with the ear of several influential senators and congressmen . . . a Nobel laureate who early on publicly endorsed a Republican platform and threw his shoulder against the wheel, before the bandwagon of recessionary fears had gained its present awesome momentum. . . .

"And through these holes we detect other radiation, masked almost everywhere by the so-called fireball haze, of a very different nature—proving that the universe is radically different in overall character from anything we thought hitherto. . . . Not only is the cosmos nonisotropic, but the whole physical universe with all the matter in it, including this earth of ours, did not hatch from a Primal Egg at all! A positive, matter universe hatched approximately ten billion years ago, certainly!—and promptly vanished into another mode of being, as soon as it had hatched! Galaxies, stars, ourselves—are only a kind of ghost of it. We have certainly detected the footsteps of God echoing in the heavens at the time of creation: but those steps are heading away from us!"

"That's laying it on pretty thick!" muttered Max, sagging further into himself, remarkably unghostlike in appearance—if somewhat amoeboid.

"It's necessary, Max, for the presentation. Even if it wasn't true."

"A quotation from *Hamlet*, perhaps?" interpolated

Max wryly. "'Oh, that this too, too solid universe would melt, thaw and resolve itself into a . . .' A what? A concatenation of micro black holes?"

Hammond tossed down his first sheet and picked up a second—which Richard noticed was blank, apart from the equations containing the hub of the argument. Typical of Dr. Paul that he had typed a grandiose overture, yet not bothered with any text to flesh out the vital part of the theorem.

"Let us imagine the primary fireball, gentlemen," he extemporized; already addressing multitudes. . . .

"Now, this primal 'Egg', into which all the matter and energy of a future universe is packed, wraps the fabric of space around itself, tightly. There is no else-where—no beyond—no other *place* for anything to exist. Then this Egg explodes. So far orthodox theory takes us. But consider the *manner* of its exploding. From Hubble's Constant (I'll explain that to them, don't worry) we must deduce that the original Egg only measured three to four light-years across. Yet within four minutes from the instant of the bang, the fireball would have grown to eighty light-years across, and six minutes after that it would have to be eight hundred light-years across. Since then, it has grown three hundred million times larger and cooled proportionately, becoming the present universe expanding at its current rate. However," he licked his lips and his eyes gleamed, "something is very wrong here."

Some people seem to talk fast on principle, reflected Richard, to impress other people with their high I.Q. Yet there are usually snickers or coughs or some trick doing duty for the normal mortal hums and haws. Not so with Paul Hammond. Once launched, he simply ran out of breath every now and then and had to glide awhile before resuming his hectic flight.

"An expansion within six minutes by a factor of seven hundred and twenty light-years supposes a figure for the speed of light of two light-years per secōnd. Which is quite impossible, unless we tinker with the concept of time itself. In this situation each particle would soon reach infinite mass, with an infinitely strong gravitational field. Thus each particle will have to collapse into a singularity. The fabric of space can't grow fast enough to contain such an explosion as the theory envisages. The only expansion must have been inward—"

"Like 'internal emigration' under the Third Reich," writhed Max.

"Precisely! Good phrase, I'll remember it. The universe emigrated internally. Leaving a myriad of extremely tiny black holes, to bond together violently to form what we call 'matter.' Such are the 'quarks'—the granules of subatomic matter—that so many million dollars have been spent vainly hunting for in the cyclotrons! This is, of course, why there's no vast mass of antimatter in the cosmos. Statistically there ought to be a fifty-fifty balance of matter and antimatter. *There was.* But all such trivial distinctions vanish in the black hole. We have a cosmos occupied almost purely by matter because it is founded on bonded shells of nothingness. But this is not, of course, the universe that was created by God. We can only speculate about what happened in the 'real' universe. And what is happening now—"

Max's hands flopped about briefly in mid-air, like flippers, before splashing back into his body again. He shut his eyes.

"Where is the real universe that God created? That exists in another dimension that all true matter and antimatter was forced into by the physics of expansion. This universe of ours is"—he brought his palms together in a mock Buddhist gesture of blessing—"an illusory by-product. *Maya*—an illusion. Illusory forms imposed on by a matrix of nothingness. The energy released by the fusion of all those singularities is what powers our expansion—not the Big Bang. Out at ten billion light-years we've detected a few glimpses of the original glory. *But it is not our glory . . .*"

He examined his well-manicured hands thoughtfully, as a set of nonexistent phenomena—those hands which caressed Ruth so unconvincingly: so sure of their own tactile supremacy.

Max shook himself—a tired seal emerging from the water. We're all turning into animals, Richard thought —his own personal troupe of them. One performing seal over there . . . And how about me? Some kind of furry teddy bear . . . Basically an inactive pet.

"This business about the speed of light being two light-years per second," Max objected. "Why not, Paul? Suppose each particle is regarded individually as having rest-mass—"

Hammond made an impatient gesture.

"The signal leakage through our 'peepholes' corresponds exactly with the proposed fusion of singularities into matter. There's no doubt about it!"

"Paul—they'll ask how we can have peepholes, when there is no 'elsewhere' to be peeped at. . . ."

"Well, even my wife's capable of asking me that one! It's easy." He ticked off the stages on his fingers. "First, there's the Egg, with all space wrapped around it. Second, this explodes in the Fireball, generating space as it expands. Third, all particles reach infinite mass, and collapse—at approximately, but *not exactly* the same time. That's the key, that fraction of overlap! Then, fourth: these singularities fuse to form what we complacently think of as matter, while the energy freed in the process powers the expansion of the resulting pseudo-cosmos—"

Hammond gazed at Richard Kimble darkly.

"The spur to all future astronomy, my dear Richard, and to religion, too, I might add, will be the crying need to understand the nature of the *real* universe that emigrated internally—in Max's touching phrase —in those first few moments of time. The true universe is, as the mystics put it, an immanent reality residing within every atom of our bodies. Yet it is on the other side of an impenetrable barrier! It must be an organized universe in itself. I have no doubts on this score. Nor that it is the actual universe intended by God!"

"Peopled with His Angels?" sighed Max. "Why must we drag religion into every equation?"

"Because science has hitherto appeared to dethrone religion! I now reinstate it. I prove the existence of God by this scenario. For the universe is a once-off universe. Where did the Primal Egg come from in the first place? From the collapse of some previous cosmos resembling ours? Oh, no! There could be no previous cycle of being, if matter is what I say it is. 'Nothing can come of nothing,' if you insist on my quoting Shakespeare. Even a fool knows that. The collapse of our present cosmos, when it occurs, cannot possibly produce another Egg—only a ravening point of void. Nothingness to the nth power!"

"It seems to me," judged Max, "that you demonstrate atheism, not religion. I mean atheism in the literal sense. The absence of God. Sure, He's somewhere. Sure, He set off the Big Bang. But we're just irrelevant to him—all our stars and galaxies."

"Nevertheless," Paul hammered home, "a God exists—even if not for us. Because there was only one universe ever made. He built a universe on the other side of ours! Physics and chemistry must be entirely different over there. Logic, too! Our task is to build a cosmology for *that* universe, now. Screw this one. That Richard should imagine this means the end of funds strikes me as amazingly shortsighted. Incidentally, no wonder that Ozma bullshit failed! There can be no radio signals from Tau Ceti or anywhere. Any advanced race has better things to do with its resources than gossiping across back fences with its neighbors."

"Paul, getting back to this idea that a God must have created the Egg, since it can only exist once in the whole of eternity . . . Surely, given infinite time, anything can happen—including the spontaneous appearance of a universe?"

"My dear Max, time is a function of matter, just as space is. There's no such thing as an 'eternity,' wait-

ing for events to occur some time, any more than
empty space exists, waiting for a universe to fill it up."

"So we simultaneously prove the existence of God,
and that he does not exist *for us*," mourned Max.
"What glad tidings to announce to the world's press!
Is it wise, Paul?"

"Should stir things up a bit," grinned Paul. "I'm getting bored with local issues. Moons, planets, milky
ways. Astronomy must become the highest form of
philosophy—indeed, of religion! It's high time people
had their minds torn away from petty squabbles about
oil and copper and fish and things." He laughed in a
cackling, zany way, glancing briefly over his shoulder.
The vulture was rooting around the rubbish pit for
chicken bones now. It would be nice to imagine,
thought Richard, that Paul simply hoped to induce a
mood of Buddhistic resignation in the world's inhabi-
tants at a time when all possible futures seemed
equally depleted, tawdry and mean.

Max said a few random things about what had
been on the radio even that morning, while they
snatched a bite of breakfast. . . . A Japanese super-
tanker had been sunk by guerrilla mines in the Straits
of Malacca . . . The anthrax epidemic, spreading from
battle-torn New Guinea, had reached Celebes and
Mindanao . . . The Australians had withdrawn their
ambassador from Washington in protest at the appearance of radioactive icebergs in Antarctic waters,
which the Australians laid at the door of the American Atomic Energy Commission's waste disposal project, Operation Icebox. . . .

Symptomatic strains on the world's temper and
sanity. . . . But Max succeeded only in sounding irrelevant and incoherent, mentioning these. What had
that got to do with cosmology?

"Can we kindly hit the hay, Paul?" he finally
begged. "Some of us are human . . . I go along with
you—give the world something else to think
about. . . . But that it must be this?" he added in a
quiet undertone of horror.

"Human, all too human," nodded Hammond gaily. "You've worked well, go and rest. For the reporters."

"I may duck out of that part, Paul. I feel tired to my bones. . . ."

"The human state," meditated Hammond, as they got up to leave. "Before, it was our own nothingness we had to come to terms with—death. From today, it will be the nothingness of matter itself—of all this cosmos. . . ."

"He reminds me of the Ancient Mariner," Richard confided. "Shall we shoot that vulture and hang it round his neck?"

"This is no joking matter," snapped Max, shutting Hammond's door upon him. "We need a really long base line for observations, to be sure. By which I mean at least one dish in earth orbit and another on the moon—"

"Which may be exactly what Paul hopes to create a furor for!" Richard exclaimed hotly, in a fit of righteous self-persuasion—reluctant, now, to identify himself with the defeated Max. "A new Apollo mission for mankind—"

"Earth's hordes need such a mission?" sneered Max. "God help us."

"Maybe Paul's right! How else can we ensure the continuity of fundamental research? The cutbacks we've seen already will be fleabites to the austerities ahead. We're only here courtesy of Paul's political wizardry. But even wizardry has its limits. If Paul has to become a prophet now to keep astronomy in business—"

"—then that's all right by you?" Max's voice, tired as it was, was contemptuous. "A new religion of a godless universe, that proves the existence of God in another mode of being—*oy veh*, Paul is crazy! He thinks this will help the world? I give up. What can an old man do . . . ?"

Max looked almost whimsical with self-mockery, then, as he slouched off to get some sleep.

Richard walked along the corridor in the opposite direction, his mind set on images of whales and the ocean; but they failed to purify him.

He stumbled outside. The sheer glare of the Mexican daylight stunned him and rang behind his eye sockets deafeningly—the bowl of blue sky a great bell, seen from the inside.

He noticed Ruth Hammond sitting on a boulder in the shade cast by the Big Dish and loped into the shade beside her, suppressing an urge to clap his hands over his ears. She was watching a mauve lizard catch flies as they settled on an empty ravioli can.

You could measure the slow rotation of the dish, as it automatically tracked signals from one of the "footsteps," by the snail's pace transit of shadows across the pitted soil. . . .

"Paul's founding a religion for himself," he said incoherently. "The First Church of Mystical Atheism, Scientist. . . . Want to join it as a groupie?"

He was too tired to decide whether he was being witty or insulting. And after that there was little more to be said.

Eleven

He dreams that he's trapped in waves of snow—a chilling softness that deafens every sound, blinds every sight. White blur, white noise . . . He tries to escape, racing away on breaching limbs. And sounds call to him from behind, trying to make sense. But the blood-beat in his ears slurs and erases them. The tetchy, panic beat of his blood makes a booming drum of his skull.

Those ghosts behind are called "words" . . .

Momentarily he halts; and opens his sensitivity up to this amorphous wilderness of the mind. Briefly, the crazy beating halts; and he almost understands those word ghosts; and why he is fleeing, and even *how* he accomplishes it—then into the echoing hollow in himself floods a soothing waxen oil, and he wakes to find himself wallowing in waves of sea, spouting out the acrid white wool of snow from his nostril as a bitter foam.

The dream scares him. In it, he was both seeing, and *not seeing* those snow waves. It was as if he was

71

inventing the shape of snow from later knowledge that had nothing to do with his dream life. . . .

Physically, he first remembers seeing snow, squinting from cold waters at rough barren shores blotted right down to the sea line by that whiteness, feeling his flukes wrench queerly at the sight of land, as he spy-hopped, thrashing about to try to stand and see.

Then, he bruised his brow and back, thrusting through floating boulders of hard chunky ice, to nuzzle at their snowcaps.

He was cold and hungry at that time, living off fat, and fleeing south.

And two tiny silver fish had darted through the sky —with a twin roll and crack smacking the waters as they turned and twisted; and they might have been sparks before his eyes, if it weren't for that sharp whipcrack of their tails! He had to roll on his side awkwardly, to see the brief flash of silver against gray. Then there was only one silver fish, and a screeching flame diving for the zone of the sea where he was.

He fled as shocks ripped through the waters, rocking ice boulders from side to side—the blow from the sky!

The surface water tasted foul, gluey and burnt. Things floated about which he nudged around, sensing that this particular "fist" was wrecked, its fingers pulled apart and broken. A limp mass of chilled flesh floated bound in soft wrappings with long streamers and a white dome of soft air. The queer divided flukes of this beast in the water—its flukes might indeed have *run*, through snow, on land. . . . Familiarity rasped at him—and foreignness, too.

"Who are you?" he'd pulsed at the tangled shape. But the small forked beast was dead. He played with it for a while, bobbing the thing about with his brow, till the bubbles popped out, and it sank.

The fist . . . it could cripple him. Burn him. Boil the oil in his brow . . .

His body once felt that itch blaze into a fire, to show him what it is, time and again. His body remembers this blazing-up of pain, but it's not a full memory. *He* didn't live through it—as he lived that flight through snow. . . .

Other memories of his body: the first gasp of air, the cloud of bloody froth, the side of the great mother shape . . . Yet *he* wasn't the one who experienced it; it filters through to him only as a body-memory, not a memory of the mind.

Early joys and agonies of his body, dawning out of that foam of blood long ago, elude him; yet every waft of his fins and twist of his flukes convey awareness of them.

A strange hiatus exists between his being born and being here. Streams of contrary Being converge on the present. So many layers of memory . . . such confusion . . .

Snow. He never saw it till much later. But now he sees it in his dream, as an experience of Before—and invents the look of it, in retrospect. Could he also invent the appearance of that "voice," of those "words"?

Categories are twisted out of shape, to accommodate his dream. Its very flimsiness is full of a pathos that torments him, as it writhes in a womb of pre-experience, aching to be born—or else aborted mercifully.

Twelve

The single bell clanged tinnily over Mezapico, as Richard Kimble sat in the pulquería facing a glass of lime refresco with some gin in it. Paul Hammond's Sierra, parked obliquely, blocked the narrow street outside. A CBS team was filming locality shots of the village, and Richard was its escort.

Several extra policemen had been drafted into the village from San Pedro. They sat across the way in full view at a table behind the still-wrecked wall of the comisaría, wearing fat black revolvers and playing cards. The CBS team reported a roadblock manned by soldiers beyond San Pedro towards the city, screening press and turning sightseers back. And these sightseers were many: four thousand people, at an estimate. A queer mix of illiterate Indian peasants, jobless industrial workers and middle-class families from the inflation-stricken city, American tourists and dropouts from over the border . . . Their numbers were still swelling. For people didn't go away. They just stayed there—arguing, drinking, huckstering, praying, demonstrating; but above all *waiting*.

The news had been out five days now, of the existence of mathematical equations proving that God existed, but that this universe was not his, only a falsehood.

Richard was wondering whether to down another mouthful of the gin fizz, which he didn't particularly care for, having ordered at random, when a Land Rover pulled up by the Sierra and began negotiating its way around the obstacle, lurching on to the mound of debris outside the comisaría. He ran out to flag the vehicle down. A floridly elaborate red windshield sticker identified the three occupants as PRENSA, press. A fat man was driving; beside him sat a tanned muscular type with handsomely sculptured features disfigured by a nasty scar puckering his right cheek, and a green military forage cap jammed down over short sun-bleached blond hair; in the back hunched a dark fawnlike presence which Richard didn't properly register at first.

"I guess we can get around," the fat man grunted, waving Richard away. Half-moons of sweat eclipsed his shirt armpits.

"No, you don't understand. I'm Dr. Hammond's assistant, Richard Kimble. I'm acting as his press officer. He's very busy obviously. I'm down here because CBS—"

"Who did you say you were?"

"Kimble. Richard Kimble. I've been working with Dr. Paul on the Footsteps of God hypothesis—"

"Hypothesis? Is there some doubt, then?" demanded the dark presence promptly, in a foreign accent, maybe Italian. Richard peered in at him. Saw there the soft fawn features of a Neapolitan street urchin who had sprung up mature with pasta and manhood, then somehow been tumbled back to his original form—as though he'd fallen into a washing machine, to emerge both more freshly innocent and sadly creased. Large brown eyes stared back accusingly at Richard.

"Observations, findings," he corrected himself, firming up. "It'll most likely be known as Hammond's Theorem. There'll be a full press briefing by Dr. Paul tomorrow. That's what we call him affectionately," he lied, feeling myth accrue even as he spoke.

"You mean we stay in this dump till then?"

"Of course not," Richard grinned at the driver. "There's accommodation on site. You'll get meals up there. Everything's arranged."

"Including armed guards," said a voice from the back.

"Yes, why the heavy security?" the front passenger asked.

"I only just heard about that, in fact. I guess it's to avoid interference. You'll only be staying a couple of days, but tourists could keep on turning up indefinitely. . . ."

"You need to shoot them, if they do?" insinuated that dark voice. "It's a preriot situation back there. It has all the ingredients."

"Gianfranco's right on that score," confirmed the fat man. "Know something, keeping folks away *provokes* hysteria, if anything. I must file a report on that roadblock scene—it's crazy."

"Oh surely you're exaggerating," Richard temporized. "Look, could we just stay here a while till CBS has done its bit? Then we'll all go up together."

"Well, seeing as you've found the local bar."

"Right," laughed Richard.

As soon as they were seated round the table inside, the Italian—whose surname was Morelli—continued talking urgently about the significance of the roadblock. He seemed obsessed by it, needling and accusing Richard Kimble. . . .

"Only, what is the riot directed against? Your telescope, for setting up this principle of emptiness as a scientific truth? Or the emptiness in their souls? Or the emptiness in their pockets? Whatever it is, your telescope focuses it! Perfectly ordinary middle-class citizens there, too. Bank clerks and tradesmen, I know the sort. A failing system—is that the key? As in Hitler's Germany? Only, all systems are no-go now. Church. State. Communism, Fascism, Democracy. For Science to spell out this message of despair is the last straw. It isn't just despair about resources or energy or foodstuffs this time. It's despair in the very concept of Being. That's the final treachery. Some vague belief in the actuality of one's own existence was the only anchor left. Call it a man's sense of authenticity." He gazed levelly at Richard. "The people have been betrayed. That's a dance of death beginning at your barricade."

"But it isn't *my* barricade!"

"Then why is it there, with soldiers?" Morelli's eyes blazed with hatred. Richard wondered whatever had made him so virulent. Loss of faith? But faith in what?

"Some fool's auto engine can show up a quasar if it doesn't have a proper suppressor fitted . . ."

The blond man—called Ivor something—barked with laughter.

"I counted six armored half-tracks and the best part of two platoons. That's protecting yourself from interference? They'd strung out hundreds of yards of barbed wire on crossbars into the scrub with a little Checkpoint Charlie in the center." The handsome golden face with its disfiguring pucker leered at Richard. "You should have seen them prancing around encouraging photos as they let us through! What fine soldiers we are!"

"It reeks of Cecil B. de Mille, on a shoestring budget," snarled Morelli. "It's been *fixed*."

"Those boys don't know what they're in for. That mob's poised to go. I've a nose for these things."

Richard mopped his brow with the back of his hand, bewildered.

"If their mood's that ugly, I guess the telescope *does* need protecting."

"I said, their mood's ugly *because* they're being frustrated," the fat man reminded. "Otherwise they'd just troop up here and gawp, most likely. But what the hell, it's good copy."

The patrón—a surly, thickset peasant—brought a tray of drinks: rum and soda for the Italian, warm beer for the other two.

"*Hielo?*" the fat man enquired hopefully. "Got any ice "

The patrón shook his head and stalked off.

"Of course he won't have any," sniggered Morelli. "There's an embargo on electrical interference, didn't you hear? So no refrigerators."

"That's not true," snapped Richard. "I resent the implication. Our technicians regularly tour the whole area fixing up God knows what gimcrack generators and other things. We even replace worn-out equipment with new for free, sometimes. We've got to. And it *costs*."

And it probably cost Paul some hefty string-pulling to arrange that military outing, too! But—Cecil B. de Mille? The soldiers obviously weren't hired extras. Yet that they had, nevertheless, been procured for the occasion, with a touch of drama in mind, seemed all too plausible. . . .

"That roadblock," he muttered apologetically. "Tell me more about it."

"You have to realize about crowd dynamics and popular movements," Morelli expounded in a fervent, didactic way. He was representing a French news agency, Richard saw from his press badge . . . but he seemed to be representing himself more than anything.

"Four distinct groups interact down there, on account of this artificial barrier. The superstitious peasant, believing that scientists have proved the existence of God—but he isn't sure whether this means the Devil rules the world, since God's apparently been on vacation ever since he made the damn thing! The petty bourgeois, already threatened on all sides by the collapse of traditional values, and well enough informed to fear the coming years deeply. He's motivated by class terror and greed—the usual prefascist mood leading on to dictatorships. Only, it could be manipulated towards a kind of Scientology. I'm using the wrong word. That's a cult that already exists. I mean some hard-science equivalent to the peasant's concept of 'salvation.' That might offer the bourgeois a way out. Call it Scientism or Scientocracy—some power-bent mysticism of Science. Then the hippie Californians are gearing up for a repeat performance of the Altamont Festival to celebrate the new revelations, banging their guitars and their girls. They're always hunting for a guru. . . ."

As Morelli talked, Richard kept visualizing the movie of *The Ten Commandments* he'd seen as a youngster. That was de Mille, wasn't it? A clip flashed before his mind's eye of Moses descending from the Mountain bearing the graven tables of the Law to the disconsolate Israelites, wailing and rioting in the scrub—and the face of Moses, with wiry silver hair swept back by the electricity of God's presence, was the face of Paul Hammond. . . .

"The nonfreak tourists, finally, represent the Middle-American bourgeoisie, even more betrayed and disenchanted by current affairs than their Mexican cousins. Bitter, too, at the shameful decline of their country. A chauvinistic upsurge of pride and dedication to something, however malignant, that revives the Spirit of Apollo will serve them. Ideally it should repolarize the scientific genius of the American people towards some abstract otherworldly goal, without the Vietnam taint attached to it. Technological, yes. But religious rather than political or military. The barrier functions as the crucible for these very diverse, yet representative ideological strains. Bayonets will be the stirring spoons. It's a potent brew: the stuff of mania on a world scale!"

How Dr. Paul would have fluffed out his feathers to hear this analysis of the situation. Richard almost believed he'd parked the Sierra the careless way he had, impromptu roadblock-style, as a reflex conditioned by Paul. . . .

But while they sat drinking, the village priest peered in hesitantly.

Abruptly he came into the pulquería, with a curious little skip, as if crossing a narrow, very deep crevasse.

His bald crumpled head seemed to have shrunken or caved in above the ears. It kept nodding from side to side like a detached skull perched loosely on top of his spinal column and only balancing there. Or as if tiny, invisible flies kept settling on it that had to be dislodged.

"*Dispénseme* . . . one of you is from the, ah, thing on the mountain, yes?" Teeth half-rotted away into brown, stained gums . . .

Richard identified himself doubtfully. The priest looked so much frailer and more pitiable than when standing by his church the other day—a discarded puppet.

"My name, ah, Father Luis. I have heard, you know, of your, ah, discovery of God's absence. *Deus absconditus* . . ." He stuck a finger in that broken mouth and pushed at his tongue; nodded. "I understand the, ah, Mezapico way—though I cannot make the right sounds with my mouth. You have to learn from childhood. But they are whistling about the soldiers down there. And the crowds—"

He gestured helplessly.

"I have to know what it means . . . I have to tell my . . . children, something, to console them. To explain. They have nothing. To say that they *are* nothing . . ." The words died.

"I have prayed that the, ah, silver thing up there would not . . ." He broke off; his words changed course. "I had a vision, you see. I have told this to no one. Not even to my superiors in San Pedro."

Wiping the sweat forcibly off his palms on to his trousers, the fat man began scribbling shorthand copy on a steno pad.

Morelli hung on Father Luis's words avidly, as if intent on memorizing them. The notion drifted through Richard's mind that if the roadblock soldiers could be regarded as hired extras in this cosmic drama of Paul's, why shouldn't this old priest have been primed to play a part, too? But it was a ridiculous idea. Father Luis, with his stumbling enunciation and his shabby revelations, whatever they were? He'd been stuck in this desert of deprivation that was Mezapico, for years. Like some third-rate St. Anthony, he had a chance to babble visions now. But he was just a sad, pathetic figure—a broken toy. How precariously his head nodded as he spoke his dribbles of speech!

"One day I went up close tō see it . . . I walked all the way there. When I reached it . . ." His cupped hands indicated the orientation of the Big Dish, angled as low as it would dip. "No one else, no other human soul alive. The whole world dead. Only carrion fowl. Sterility. Waste."

"The valley of dry bones," glossed Richard promptly. It was all so derivative. What was it? Ezekiel—or Ecclesiastes? He forgot. But didn't this prove that Dr. Paul had no possible connection with the priest? Paul, tricked out in his albatross, would have dreamed up a less banal tale to buttonhole travelers with, than an obvious Bible tract.

"But what is special about that?" Father Luis exclaimed, staring hard at Richard in apparent denial of his suspicions. "It is all around us here. That was merely my *mood*. A mood is different from a vision—

"Ah, my vision! The silver bowl hung tipped toward me. It was filled with light, a spoonful of the sun. But instead of spilling out of the bowl, this liquid hung . . . vertical. It defied the earth's pull. Its own pull was stronger. Have you seen a foundry? Watched the bowls of molten metal pouring out as lava from a volcano? Yet this molten light would not pour out! There was no heat, only light. Yet how *strong* this light was!"

Clenching his frail fist, he set the finger joints crackling and trembling as though intent on making them fall to dust.

"I do not mean that it blinded me, no—not strong in that way. But strong like . . ." His fist flapped limply, unable to conjure up the gesture again. "*Sinews*. A creature all of bright sinews. Every moment it drew in more muscles of light from the breast of the sun. And that light-creature swam stiffly within itself, tensing its stolen fibers. But then its, ah, its grip upon itself became so fierce, so powerful . . . How greedily it wrapped itself in those fibers! Already it had sucked all the sinews of the sun into itself, so that the sun stood black beside me—drained as though by some terrible torture . . . not flaying but worse . . . all the muscles drawn out of the body like wires till the body is a useless inert mass blazing with agony."

"The reason for the sun going dark," Richard gabbled at the others, "is obviously all this staring he was doing at the reflection in the dish with his back to the real sun! The light receptors in the center of the retina get jammed 'open'—and the side receptors are only for detecting change and motion. There wasn't any change, the way he was staring, so they switched off. So he got the illusion of staring vertically down a tunnel of light! You can duplicate the effect yourselves . . ."

"Shut your idle chatter," hissed Morelli.

"Do you really angle your telescope directly at the sun?" inquired the blond man, with amused incredulity. "No wonder it gets spots before its eyes!"

Richard found he couldn't work out what the respective positions of telescope, priest, and sun, must have been, when he came to think of it. . . . The Big Dish couldn't have been pointing directly at the sun; the man was right.

Ah—the old priest was probably half-blind, in any case! His hesitation before crossing the threshold into the bar was that of a man who couldn't see anything inside the shaded room; who took the existence of a solid floor within on faith—though that faith had to be wound up like a piece of clockwork to activate it.

Father Luis resumed with a disconsolate shrug. Not a shrug of tolerance or patience, however. Time had somehow ceased to exist for him; there was no context for patience or impatience to occur in.

"The sinew-being . . . it started to consume itself, as it had already consumed all the fibers of the sun.

Torturning itself now, it sucked and gutted itself of light. The beast swallowed itself, and I couldn't see a being any more. Nor anything whatever. I hung with my feet on nothing, then. My eyes beheld nothing. I was dying, I knew, being sucked into the void. But!" He popped his finger in his brown, eroded mouth again and pushed his tongue. This time he succeeded in summoning up a wheezing squeak, as he mimed . . .

"Whistling was all around me, like calls of birds—snatching me back, building the world again. Three Indians whistling into the silver bowl, and the muscles of sound they blew, drew me back! They remade the world for me. So I could see it. Though it did not wholly exist, I also knew that. My faith changed then . . . It is the thoughts and speech of man that make the world, not the thoughts of God. Man is not a thought in the mind of God; but the opposite: the world is a thought in man's mind. Please," he begged, his head nodding in exhaustion as if he would go to sleep standing before them, "do not *unthink* the world. It is a poor, rotten desert, this, but it is a home of souls, too. . . .

"So I am ringing the bell because that is the only way I can . . . whistle. . . ."

Morelli stared after Father Luis, entranced, as the priest ducked abruptly back into the sunshine baking the street—plucked by the sinews of light. . . .

Richard shivered violently.

But by then the CBS film crew had drawn up in its hired Land Rover and were blaring their horn impatiently.

Thirteen

How these ghosts from an unreal life mock him, make an idiot of him!

Again he nuzzles up against a female of the harem; slides along her side, rubbing his hide against hers, caressing her with his flippers. How he yearns to dive beneath her, corkscrew round her, dance with her, thrash the sea together. How he aches to race and rear up out of the waters with her, balancing in each other's clasp on the ocean before crashing back in spray and spume. How his penis sings to enter her in that fleeting climax as they stand upright on the waves together—he pulsing his love into her, as his mother pulsed milk into someone resembling him once—and as he pulses signals into the air, to release that fearful itch!

Orgasm was a less precarious balancing business once—with a less frenzied need to seize it on the crest of breaking, yielding waves. . . .

Orgasm was by way of a slow lying down together, twining of limbs he cannot understand, impossible touch of mouths and tongues. Hair flowed around him like seaweed, adhering, clinging. . . .

Thus he disregards the true message of his clicks, for the sake of a fantasy. Foolishly he ignores the hard bubble of flatulence in her belly—the swollen flesh in her womb—the hard knot deeper in her bowels that will perfume the sea when she voids it, which discomforts her now: all spelling out—UNAVAILABILITY! All these signs that he reads through her soft walls, echo-mapped upon his melon, he pays scant heed to—obsessed, frustrated—as much by the craving to know himself as by any urge to know her, sexually.

His "fingers" had played, in darkness, upon an invisible body, indecipherable to him apart from by touch, and by the hard dull bark of "words" . . .

The furious thrashing of the waves! The angry twisting! He disregards them. Discards the knowledge that she doesn't care to dance on the sea with him.

He only half-hears the snare-drumming of threatening clicks—the tetchy, abrasive, exasperated challenge.

Then the Great Bull lobtails and is hundreds of feet below, rising beneath him, not in love, but *like a fist!*

The blow comes close to staving in his ribs. His flipper agonizes, as the Bull's jaws seize it and wrench it this way and that; discarding it like offal, spitting it out contemptuously—an aching, living offal, still a living part of him, though he can only tell that from the pain. . . .

Into his brow is pulsed, in rage, the simplest, most babyish glyph of all: INCONGRUENCE!

He is a fool. A pup with half a mind.

Fourteen

Paul Hammond threw a triumphal barbecue party that evening, under the blaze of stars, for all the visiting newsmen and resident technicians, at which Ruth presided with a great-lady air, Paul apparently having laundered and groomed her in Richard's absence. She wore a dress he'd never seen before, or even imagined her capable of wearing. Inset with hundreds of tiny mirrors, it captured the firelight and lamplight in mockery of the stars above. Ruth was her own milky way, her own spiral galaxy spinning at a vastly speeded up rate, as she moved about among reporters and cameramen who were getting steadily drunker—abetted by a Dr. Paul who stayed cold sober, while he encouraged them to copy some of the orgy spirit of events down on the desert plain. From this mountain height, a bonfire that must have been huge indeed glowed far away beyond San Pedro on the road to the city—a winking orange star of the first magnitude.

Once, they heard what might have been a rattle of gunfire, far away, trapped and amplified by the Big

Dish. It could have been somebody trampling on dry sticks beyond the circle of light—an Indian, maybe, watching the party; or a vulture, stamping impatiently and clacking its wings for the lamb being roasted. The blond man was sure it was gunfire. After Asia, Africa and the Middle East, he should know how to estimate weaponry well enough, he boasted. He'd spent half his life as a connoisseur of gunfire, near and far, bearing the mark of his one mis-estimate on his cheek.

That clicking crackle came in a moment of absurd stillness, when even the barbecue fire and the roast had fallen into a noise trough. Everyone had stopped talking all together. They might all have been waiting for the sound . . . wishing for it.

After the second hour, when everyone was pretty well drunk, Ruth slipped away in the direction of the Hammond bungalow. Richard followed, tipsily, though he hadn't been invited—a scab of lust in him tingling to be scratched, to banish memories of Father Luis and his mumblings. They'd left a furry deposit in his mind, as though he'd been unable to brush his teeth for a few days.

Someone in the shadows was dogging his footsteps; drunkenly, he paid no attention.

Blundering quietly into the bungalow, he felt his way along the corridor towards Ruth's room. A faint light was showing underneath her door. Somewhere else in the house, presumably, Consuela was babysitting Alice; he didn't knock before opening the door.

The blond man was in bed with Ruth. Her dress lay on the floor, a discarded snakeskin with spangly scales. . . .

Supporting his bulk on one elbow, while his free hand clutched under her, the man's buttocks pumped to and fro through the thin hoop of her legs. She lay like a ballet dancer in a cambré, passé position bent through ninety degrees at the hips, her nails raking the newsman's buttocks while her other hand squeezed his scrotum gently, as if it was a plastic ketchup bottle. . . .

She opened her eyes briefly on Richard, then she closed them again as the hoop of her legs tightened round the man; only after a long interval relaxing and unlocking her companion.

The blond man rolled off her lazily, and noticed Richard. He seemed unperturbed.

"But why him?" Richard gasped, feeling more betrayed than a husband would.

Abruptly, Ruth looked disgusted and tried to tug the sheet across herself; but the man's weight was on it. It only hid her legs and the dark rhombus of her crotch, leaving her breasts bare. She was staring past Richard, out of the doorway.

He turned, to follow her eyes.

Morelli had followed him into the house. The Italian stood a little way back in the dark of the corridor. He moved forward now, as though invited by Ruth's gaze. Ignoring the woman's body, he stared only at her face—and even then, at her face as a formless unit, not at eyes or mouth. Her features might have been smeared into flat uniformity by a stocking mask, his diffuse gaze implied.

"Hammond's high priestess, then, the temple prostitute?" he inquired softly. "It figures."

The blond man rolled over to secure a pack of Kools from his shirt on the floor.

"Don't pay any attention to him, Mrs. Hammond. He's just jealous because his balls got wrecked by an Arab land mine. He used to be the perfect trendy Marxist lady-fucker once. Don't I know it! Sexuality and the class struggle, you should have heard him. But he's reverted to a sort of prepubertal state since then, you see. Eh, Gianfranco? Catholic sin and all that—but still somehow missing the softness of Mother Church's bosom?"

Morelli took this exposure surprisingly calmly; or else, his private pain was instantly shunted off elsewhere, along a well-worn course. He just bowed drolly, and withdrew, leaving the two men alone with Ruth, and Ruth with her back to them, sobbing.

"Fuck off!" she swore, facelessly. "Get out of here all of you! This isn't a sideshow. I'm real. I hate you—"

Paul Hammond appeared at nine the next morning for the official news conference and filmed interviews in the shade of the Big Dish; calm and alert, conducting every word and gesture with inspired panache. . . . To the various hangovers present, no doubt doubly impressive. Having descended from his mountain to revel in the plain by proxy the previous evening, he'd reascended to the empyrean. Down on the real plain, meanwhile, far away, a thin column of black smoke rose up for perhaps a thousand feet before meeting an inversion layer which squashed it out to the four points of the compass in the breathless air, creating a tall thin-stemmed fungoid tree.

Morelli's questions were to upset Hammond, however.

They weren't so much questions, in the event, as a fundamental, reasoned declaration of opposition. The Italian may have been brooding Father Luis's words too, reflected Richard, as an alternative to raking over last night's embers—yet it was plain that he'd done his scientific spadework before ever arriving in Mezapico. Now he addressed Hammond as an equal—as though they were coparticipants in the Seattle conference—an approach that plainly dislocated Dr. Paul's mental schedule. Recalling Paul's dismissal of journalists as "uninformed," Richard felt savagely amused.

"I am thinking, Dr. Hammond," Morelli began his indictment primly, "about the value of *believing* in reality. You are in effect denying authenticity to the universe, correct? Yet doesn't modern physics say that the observer plays a role in creating the reality he observes? That he is by no means neutral? I'm wondering if, let's say, the Schrödinger Cat Paradox isn't necessarily true of the universe as a whole? The paradox that we—the human race, as a consensus of observers—are every moment engaged in choosing the type of universe we inhabit. We must choose, and what we choose will come into being, *so!*" He snapped his fingers. "At every moment of every day we are collectively free to choose, so it is human *practice* that makes the world what it is. We participate. This isn't Marxism or mysticism, Dr. Hammond —but physics, surely?"

"You mean that crap about biological factors selecting the physical constants of the universe? To observe a universe at all, you need living observers—life—so a universe has to be compatible with the evolution of life. Otherwise no observers, hence no universe The universe is as-it-is because we're here? Yes, I know the idea. It's a logic loop. It hasn't got anything to do with the daily running of the universe. I don't see what you mean by us choosing our universe every moment. Do *you*, for that matter?"

"Yes, I think so. There's a very queer interface between reality and ourselves; let's be honest. Things are by no means as plain as common sense might suggest. We participate, right? But what if the human race decrees an illogical, irrational choice? And our choice is incompatible with life and common sense? Then life can't have arisen in such a universe, to observe it. We would be lost then, indeed! Erased by our own folly. For observable 'universes' are not illogical. Suppose we become irrational, will we simply vanish, leaving the owls and otters, deer and monkeys of the earth to sustain reality, till a new higher intelligence arises? Or can we pull all reality down with us? This rare, beautiful reality!"

His gesture took in the sun-battered landscape of Mezapico—the rocks, the scrub, the smoke on the plain, the sword-gleam of the sea. Briefly it seemed to Richard that this desolation was indeed transfigured, given a fresh coat of varnish.

"What nonsense!" Hammond snapped angrily. "You're confusing two entirely different things in the typical way of amateurs—probability theory, which only deals with the behavior of individual atomic particles, and some Cosmic Theory of Parallel Universes, which is sheer mathematical speculation. . . ."

Be honest—there's more to it than that, Paul, thought Richard. . . .

"Well, the universe may reflect our own existence, okay," Paul conceded, seeing how a bad impression was being made on the other journalists, who rather relished the baiting of a Great Man, though they resented the mauling of one of their own number. "But only in the sense that we wouldn't see it, if we weren't here. But that doesn't mean we create the damn thing!"

"No, I don't think I am confusing things, Dr. Hammond," the Italian insisted, the thin passion of his voice a worm boring through stone with acid bites. "Probability theory and cosmic theory have to be united, surely? The universe is a unity, you agree? Your own theory—this Footsteps thing—is a unified theory, isn't it? It dismisses atomic particles and galaxies alike into the same limbo, for the same reason!"

Dr. Paul nodded brusquely, half-turning away.

"Think of Schrödinger's cat, Dr. Hammond!"

"It's hardly the place or the time, Signor Morelli, to speak of cats! I may be something of an authority on catastrophes, but I'm afraid your humble pussycat leaves me cold."

His joke failed to raise a laugh.

"But this *is* the time, sir!" Morelli protested. "You have chosen to announce your news this way. And my readers don't wish to wait another whole month for the proper scientific account. No indeed, sir, other reporters may prefer a glib dismissal of the universe, not I!" Morelli glared at the blond, scarred reporter, who looked bored and lit a cigarette.

"It is a reasonable question, Paul," Max Berg adjudicated quietly, provoking Hammond to one of his abrupt chopped-off yawns: displacement behavior for biting his colleague's head off. Paul had pressured Max to put in an appearance, believing him safely tamed, and was now regretting it. "Personally I should like to hear Mr. Morelli elaborate—"

"Thank you," Morelli acknowledged, in a singularly

poisonous tone. "You will correct me if I make mistakes, gentlemen? I am after all only an amateur. So then, the great physicist Schrödinger asked what must happen if you lock a cat in a room with a flask of prussic acid and a hammer that will smash the flash automatically when a Geiger counter registers any radioactivity, correct? And beside this Geiger counter you place a certain quantity of radioactive substance, measured exactly so that there is a fifty-fifty chance that within one hour one of the nuclei will decay, thus leading to the death of the cat. At the end of that hour, what is the situation, mathematically speaking?" he demanded of Max, who was teasing his moustache hairs into his mouth, and tugging, with all the furtive defiance of somebody picking their teeth in public.

Max chewed on the question.

"We'd have to say that after one hour the total wave function for the room-cat system has a form in which live cat and dead cat are mixed in equal parts...."

"The cat must be simultaneously both alive and dead—isn't that so?"

"Mathematically, it's so," nodded Max. "Of course, in practice, the cat either lives or dies...."

"In *practice*, yes indeed! But what decides 'practice'? That is what we must discover! So then, we can say this cat inhabits two simultaneous, noninteracting worlds—which are nevertheless both *real worlds* for the scientist. Thus the simplest event on the atomic level—the radioactive decay of one nucleus—brings a whole alternative dimension into being. And this paradox is at the heart not only of quantum physics, but the physics of whole worlds: of all reality!"

"Schrödinger's puzzle," sighed Max. "You take it to its logical conclusion, you end up with every quantum event in the whole universe giving rise to copies of the entire universe every moment—"

"Including copies of the earth, including copies of ourselves! Including even—nonsense universes?"

"An infinity of universes branching into being every second, *oy veh* . . . Alice in Wonderland is simpler." Max shrugged. "But it's plausible, mathematically—"

"There was *one* creation of *one* universe," thundered Paul Hammond, "by a God who has departed. Our observations indicate this indisputably, Morelli."

"But Dr. Hammond," Morelli insisted, "of course there is always *one* universe—for the observer! Yet universes are branching into being all the time, your colleague has said so. What is it that decides which way *we* shall branch? Which universe we shall continue in? Is it sheer chance? Why, then our universe could turn into nonsense any moment—for some of the set of universes that are generated must surely be irrational universes, where time may flow backwards, where light is slower than sound, where the law is that there is no law! Observerless universes. What keeps us on a rational track? I submit that it is the human act of choice, human *practice*, that upholds reality, as surely as human choice slays or saves Schrödinger's cat. The determining factor in the cat paradox is the consciousness of the observer—that is the only active variable, yes?"

Max tore at his moustache and nodded grimly.

"So then, the observer triggers the choice. He determines what situation shall exist. Well, as below, so above. As on the microscopic level, so on the telescopic! I say the world remains as it is because of the consensus belief of all the human race that a table is a table, that the night is dark, that reality has a certain form."

Paul Hammond snorted.

"You might as well say that for as long as people thought the earth was flat and the sun went around it, that was the case!"

"I'm not speaking about mythologies, sir. I mean the general grassroots *texture* of reality...."

"So what made the choice for us, pray, before the human race evolved?" queried Hammond archly. "Eh, answer that."

"Other life forms maybe," Morelli muttered mysteriously.

"What life forms?" hooted Hammond. "Aliens? Or dinosaurs? Before the first unicellular organism even appeared on the scene, what made it tick, eh? For billions of years, too!"

"Maybe the inertia of nature? Maybe inertia prevails until there are observers? Surely the appearance of intelligence, of life itself, overturns one prime rule of the universe—of entropy, of progressive disorder, doesn't it? So life and intelligence ought not to come about. It is irrational. That may be the critical, and random, event that locks our universe into place as a *participatory one*. When the first molecule became a message, arbitrarily—generating the branch towards vital organization, no? After that, a principle of conservation of rationality prevails, unless the participant totally betrays it! No one can explain why life was. Yet in becoming proto-life, that first molecule switched the rules, and froze that change in place, in the structure of Being, statistically. And now that life *is*, what matters is the act of choice we make now. This is one of the few times in history, I truly believe, when consensus reality is both unified enough, and frail enough, to fall!"

Yawning violently, Hammond clapped his jaw shut—a lizard gulping a fly. Morelli wasn't to be gulped, however.

"You're tampering with the reality of the human race, with this negative nihilistic universe of yours," the Italian jibed. "You can even bring this falsehood into being, because our minds are so sick with worry and uncertainty. Then your universe will indeed be *the* universe. And science—*your* science—will be the religion of that empty-hearted cosmos. You will be its—"

"Quiet, damn you!" shouted Dr. Paul in a fury.

"—its Devil."

Hammond gawped. He had, indeed, been expecting the word "God."

A long silence supervened, broken only by a sudden flapping of wings as a vulture dropped from its high roost, thinking they had all gone away, leaving the rubbish pit free. Creaking with annoyance, it landed on another spar instead.

Paul Hammond gathered his wits.

"One prime objection to that rigmarole, my friend, even ignoring your amateur distortions of a thing as sophisticated as quantum physics—"

"And how about you?" Morelli shouted back. "Do you expect the majority of people not to distort? Oh, you are longing for them to distort *reality!*"

"Even disregarding your distortions," Dr. Paul pressed on testily, "this so-called branching could only involve changes from now on. From the now-situation. It couldn't alter the past. It couldn't alter the form of the Big Bang. Or before that. We can't change the past, my dear fellow, only the future—"

He turned his back on Morelli, gazing up at the dish in a photogenic pose that several cameramen swiftly took advantage of.

"I don't know if it's so Q.E.D. as all that, Paul," Richard found himself saying, out of sympathy for the fierce eunuch Italian. "What happened in the past is only happening *now* from our point of view, here on this planet. Because the information is reaching us only now. So in a sense Morelli's right, we *are* the current observers—"

"Bravo," laughed Morelli. "Thanks for small mercies, Kimble."

Dr. Paul directed a gaze of blank dislike at Richard, casting him into nonexistence; then hurried on to terminate the press briefing.

"This is all quibbling over details, gentlemen. The basic facts are as I outlined. You've all received the Xeroxed handout. I throw these ideas out into the world arena a month before Seattle, so that the world may reach its own concensus about my idea. This is a major breakthrough in our understanding of the universe. Indeed *the* major breakthrough since . . ." He groped, visibly: his grin twisted and sickly. Theatrical makeup melting from his features in the heat? He wasn't wearing any makeup . . .

Einstein? Too close, thought Richard. Copernicus, too remote. I bet he plumps for Newton.

". . . since Aristotle."

Morelli was watching Richard with wry expectancy, having intuited something about the other man's own sense of frustration from the incident in Ruth's bedroom. He expected him to act. To stem Hammond's arrogance. To attack his cosmology. Yet something stopped Richard from saying anything. Richard had internalized Paul Hammond's nihilism—absorbed it into his bloodstream. Matter was nothing: therefore, nothing was the matter. Richard smiled at his cheap pun; then felt nauseated as hangover surged over him in a dazing wave. The world's firm outlines blurred and smeared. The dish spun around his head.

To Paul Hammond's intense satisfaction, Richard Kimble had fainted.

For the majority of the newsmen, this only underlined the drama and awesomeness of the Hammond Theorem—that one of his own staff should faint at the implications, when these fully dawned on him.

Fifteen

"If only," confided Orville Parr, as the black Toyota bore Gerry Mercer and himself, *muzhik* and child, towards Kujirajima, "the kid wasn't so damn cryptic. He can only quarter-communicate even in his native Russian. So his vocabulary's beyond what you'd expect of a six-year-old! Big deal. It's still chaotic."

He lowered his voice, so that Mikhail would have difficulty hearing.

"Somebody's hidden a message in him for us to find."

The scenic highway, carved out of rumpled cascades of frozen lava, was scantily clad in pines and maples. Flashes of blue water gleamed through the trees, then a broad expanse of sea dotted with knobbly black islands and fishing boats flying bright red and blue pennants. A concrete parking lot held a tourist bus, with picnickers scooping fast mouthfuls of rice and pickles out of their lunchboxes. Thousands of disposable chopsticks littered the lot: a scurf printed with tire tracks . . .

"That's why I don't like this time limit," Parr whispered. "I'd feel far happier if we had the kid in the States, and a few months to spend on him. The Soviets are trying to stampede us. Actually adjourning a fisheries conference when half the world's going hungry, just to get a schizo kid and a halfwit muscleman back! They're *hoping* we'll dig out whatever they've brainwashed the kid into believing—and fast. Otherwise, whatever they've put into him won't hold up long. And they know it!'"

"We've been through this a hundred times, Orville. You're too . . ." Gerry hesitated, then stared mutely out to sea. Parr mentally supplied a series of missing words . . . skeptical; unimaginative; chicken . . . Which would it be?

"I guess we have to accept practicalities," he said quickly, to forestall Gerry. "Enozawa's collective wisdom has given us a week to get something substantial out of the boy—and that's all we've got to play with."

"It's a damn shame we can't take him anywhere, except in Japanese transport with a Japanese courier—"

"What difference would it make if we could? You've got to face it, Gerry—we don't pull the political muscle we used to."

"That doesn't mean our hands are tied, exactly!"

"No, you can still fly Russian kids you've fished out of the sea halfway across Japan and lock them up in airbases!"

"You still sore about that?"

But Gerry was arguing in whispers too, by now.

Mikhail might (in Parr's mind!) be a Russian agent speaking fluent English. Or might not. The Japanese chauffeur certainly did, and reported whatever he overheard to some ambiguous superiors. On that point Parr and Mercer both agreed.

The Toyota behind them bore Enozawa, with Tom Winterburn escorting Chloe Patton and Herb Flynn from the San Diego Naval Undersea Center. They'd flown in the day before. Chloe Patton had an old acquaintanceship to renew at the Whale Research

Institute on Kujirajima, apparently, with Dr. Kato, the director. "She mightn't be the brightest cookie in the world," a voice had confided to Parr over the phone from San Diego, "but that old guy has a soft spot for her. She was on an exchange scholarship to Japan, you see. . . ."

Bob Pasko should already have arrived, earlier in the day, to brief Kato on the Nilin problem.

Kujirajima—Whale Island—is reached by a long bridge causeway jutting out from the fishing port of Matsusaki—Pine Tree Cape—to a rugged lava cone a half-mile offshore. The black Toyotas threaded their way along quays where tuna boats were about to set off on their long hunt in the Pacific.

How gay they looked, thought Chloe—long bright banners running up the masts, white streamers fluttering to the quayside, where loudspeakers were jangling the Japanese hit parade over coils of tarred ropes and stalls of the comic-book vendors, where families were grouped saying good-bye.

Then they rounded a block of warehouses and came upon tuna being unloaded from a ship newly returned. A refrigerated truck gaped open at the back, to swallow the blunt blue cylinders the fish had been chopped down to. Ice-hard metal torpedoes skidded along the quay, veils of steam boiling off in the sunlight. The porters handled these frozen carcasses as fast as possible, booting them along or skidding them on their way with gaffs to the weighing platform by the truck, which they were hefted on, and off again on to a forklift in a single bounce.

Hundreds of browning mackerel dried in the sun beside more stalls, split open like fans on rows of lattices . . .

The mood of frantic *use* of the sea appalled Chloe mildly, as the car rocked along, alternately braking and accelerating till she felt like a gangster on a heist. The open comic books on the stalls revealed flash images of jagged red and black drawings of raped women, robot monsters, pistol whippings . . .

It all seemed so picturesque the last time she visited this port: a bewilderment of colors, shapes and smells. It was sinister now. The atmosphere violent, anxious and furtive—as if these ships might be setting out on their last fishing trip, and after that was . . . Hadn't there been riots only weeks before, about the steep rise in mercury levels of the Pacific tuna? The porters that spun those steaming blue corpses on their way to the markets were handling contaminated material. They only wanted it off their hands. . . . They gashed the fish the way the gangsters in the comic books gashed their molls, with sharp gaffs in place of razors.

Chloe Patton, at twenty-six, a dumpy blonde with short curly locks, hated the name Chloe and infinitely preferred being called Miss Patton. "Chloe" was the quintessential Disney goldfish, all fat and fins.

Alas, swimming around in the dolphin pens with face mask and flippers on, in her bright red dotted bikini, she gave precisely this impression.

Chloe enjoyed a beautiful rapport with the dolphins of San Diego. Maybe her cetacean charisma sprang from her contours—the sense they had of her in the water as a comic rubbery toy. Or maybe it was her guilelessness, for she hardly inquired where her dolphins went, after they'd been trained to wear snout harnesses and poke long spikes into a target; and clamp magnetic discs onto squares of different alloys. Distantly she was aware of the electrodes being implanted in their brains and in the brains of killer whales; that tiny surges of current could induce a transcendental mental experience, a thousand orgasms— or the agonies of hell. But these were only expedients, to speed up the learning of their games. Teaching aids. Few dolphins seemed to bear a grudge afterward, though one or two surly individuals deliberately lost their appetite every year, and died. . . . She mourned them sincerely.

At college she'd studied the cetacean brain microscopically by Golgi and silver impregnation techniques, without ever asking where the slides came from. She'd been the darling cheerleader of her football team, rubbery curves jouncing pneumatically as she pogoed up and down—while others held rallies against "The War," a topic she preferred not to think about. She approached cetacean psychology with the same cheerful bounce, her own cute brain only very recently stained by a few uncertainties; these might easily be confused with the first faint streaks of hysteria at finally realizing that she was sexually a comic animation, beloved of dolphins perhaps, but fancied only by old men, by kinky men, by men with something wrong with them—like Herb Flynn.

Herb's face was red and bobbly with a plague of eczema blemishes. He wore a straggly confusion of beard and tangled sideboards to cosmetize this. The harvest of hair still sprouted out of a livid, blotched soil, however. His room at San Diego was packed with jars of skin lotions. He never took to the water, staying in the operating theater and laboratories where the electrode inserts and postmortems were carried out. . . . Never having seen him with even his shirt off, she wondered whether his whole body was undergoing a perpetual acne attack. At nights she dreamed that all his skin was infested by a host of tiny jellyfish, their sting cells leaving welts on face and body alike. . . .

The thought of going to bed with him . . . the idea of those pink welts crawling off him in the dark and *investigating* her! (It would have to be in the dark, she was sure—to prevent her from seeing.) Dolphins, nudging her round the pool like a beachball, playing with her, squealing at her, riding her on their rippling laminar backs, were infinitely sexier. Herb had taken one special favorite once and cut it up, out of jealousy. She hoped this trip wouldn't throw them together too violently. Herb was contact-adhesive, with all his welts and suckers. . . .

"I've been thinking this business over very carefully," Tom Winterburn said, scratching the tip of his thin bluish nose, which protruded almost far enough for him to see its end without going cross-eyed, "and if it involves anything at all, I'd say there has to be some kind of 'transplant of consciousness' effect. . . ."

"Which is just another way of avoiding using the phrase 'mind-transfer', Tom," Flynn responded glumly, thinking of all his stereotaxic maps of dolphin brains. Sensation centers here, motor controls there . . . Such complexity, even on the conditioned reflex level! "What's a 'mind', anyway?" he demanded. "It's simply a particular brain in operation. The working mode of the brain. If a brain exceeds the thousand-gram threshold level, we can posit a 'mind' as the working mode instead of just a bundle of automatic instinctual programs—as Lilly did. But that doesn't demonstrate a mind or separate it from the body, except semantically. The rest is sheer mysticism. Do you suppose the Soviets have achieved some breakthrough on the astral plane? A disembodied mind, that can be physically reembodied? The dream of religions down the ages? I think it's highly unlikely." He halted a moment. "Alternatively, do you mean an actual brain transplant? It's been done on a crude level from monkey to monkey. I guess it could be done with a human being, though the adult human brain's much bigger than a kid's. The skull would have to be surgically enlarged. There's no sign of that on Nilin. Why use a kid at all? Surely there should be enough adult cretins in mental hospitals . . ." He petered out, as the suggestion sounded unacceptable, put in those words.

"Maybe it's a problem of adjustment?" suggested Winterburn. "Brain and body are too well integrated beyond a certain age? So you need a young host."

"But that hasn't been done! That kid still has a kid's brain in his skull. It's his own original brain matter. . . . Anyhow, the whole notion of transplanting a human brain into a whale's body is ridiculous! The human brain simply isn't designed to operate a whale anatomy. It would be like expecting a monkey to fly a jumbo jet."

"Their choice of a cosmonaut?" Enozawa queried. "Significant?"

Flynn shook his heavy, flushed head. An ape's pink matted ass, the Japanese thought to himself.

"On the contrary! That only goes to show they had nothing better to do with a crippled spaceman! Otherwise they'd have saved him for the whale job, not squandered him on the kid!"

The Toyota swung away from the shore along the causeway toward the island, negotiating its way by fits and starts through the knots of day trippers who were marching toward the lava beaches, aquariums and other sideshows.

From across the bay, occasional oily smells wafted from the whale yards. A smoke cloud of gulls milled about—ducking, diving, snatching, in an amorphous wool blob, which the sharp island peak cut off from view as it rose up before them.

"I wasn't thinking of actually transposing *brains*," Winterburn explained. "Why do they have that computer at Ozerskiy? I mean, at Nagahama," he offered the Japanese with a pucker of the lips—a bar-girl offering some rice-cracker knicknack. Enozawa acknowledged the gesture evasively. It struck him as offensively patronizing.

"That computer has a massive capacity. Now, no computer yet can match the capacity of the human brain. But perhaps this one's equal to a stripped-down version—to an abbreviated mathematical model of mind? The Nilin boy and his *muzhik* talk in terms of printing minds, don't they? We took it to mean they're printing new information into a brainwashed subject. But what if we take it literally? In that case the Russians have devised a workable mathematical scheme for describing the processes we sum up as 'mind' or 'consciousness.' You yourself said, Herb, there's no such thing as 'mind-in-general'—only the behavior of a particular brain. So it's a particular individual they must

make a model of. They need a Nilin. Preferably someone with a well-coordinated intelligence and a fairly
tough mentality!"

Flynn shook his head disbelievingly.

"When the obvious answers have all been ruled out,"
persisted the naval attaché, "the impossible answer
must be the right one."

"You sound like that lunatic Hammond!" Flynn shot
back at him, with a venom that astonished Tom Winterburn. "Well, I mean to say! Almost his exact words.
The impossibility of reality, the reality of impossibili-
ties. Our new faith, so it seems!"

"I haven't really been following the news from Mexico. Too wrapped up in this thing, I guess—"

"Lucky you!"

Chloe fluttered nervously. San Diego was so close to
the border. Not a day's drive away from that barricade, and the *orgy* going on before it. Closer still to
Tijuana, Madsville of the old days, now deliriously
reinfected. The moment she'd stepped outside the
guarded perimeter of the undersea center she'd felt
she was deserting sanity. Felt vulnerable. Out in the
open. Exposed. The frenzy of the Japanese quayside
did little to allay her fears. They too had altered: from
the picturesque to the appalling . . . The San Diego
center, whatever Herb did in his labs, was a pure Dis-
neyland oasis beside the world that began at its
gates.

The whole planet seemed to be descending into a
dark oceanic cleft in a flimsy bathysphere.

The daily news was bad enough: the war in New
Guinea, the starvation in Africa. Anthrax. Radioactivity. Now this Hammond man popping up again
with his horror story from the edge of the universe . . .

However hard she tried to thrust such things aside,
they seemed always to come bouncing back again, as
if some gremlin were playing Ping-Pong inside her
head.

"Something ought to be done about that Hammond,
Tom! He's a menace. A plague. He's the big epidemic

W.H.O.'s been scared of. Only it broke out in Mexico in a fellow's mind, not in Africa. We'd be better advised doing something about him. Take a detachment of marines down there, maybe. Whales can wait—"

Enozawa sucked in his breath sharply. After making so much fuss about keeping the Russian child! With the Japanese foreign ministry issuing bland obfuscations to the Soviet embassy, at the same time as the resources ministry were circulating increasingly tetchy memoranda about the delay. Consensus, precarious at the best of times, was as ill-balanced currently as a novice first time out on the practice mat. The only factor restraining the powerful resources ministry was this still ill-defined threat of some Soviet-programmed leviathan, or fleet of them, whose function remained a mystery. If it was only a threat to American submarines, what affair of theirs was that?

This Hammond though . . . A disconcerting man! A Nobel laureate was a kind of samurai of science, wasn't he? A samurai was accustomed to confronting blackest night and finding the flame of honor burning in its depths, as the high point of all his days: that mystical moment when he stretched out his hand to take the *seppuku* dagger. *Seppuku* had been ridiculed for decades, till Mishima once more made glorious that moment when the great man faces nothingness . . . Americans hadn't the strength in their stomachs to confront nothingness. Most Americans. This Hammond was the exception. The reaction of ordinary Americans to him proved it.

Enozawa relaxed against the black leatherette, calmed by clear images of Yukio Mishima on that balcony at Ichigaya Barracks. He had witnessed it, at least! Acting properly nowadays, he could erase the shame of his own past slovenliness.

"It mightn't be necessary to transfer the physical brain, you see," the American captain was saying. "If a mathematical model of sufficient complexity could be built up and superimposed, by some imprinting procedure . . . I guess this would have to be electrical—"

"We are here," announced Enozawa, as the car ahead pulled up at the end of the causeway. A cobbled pathway led on from here up to the top of the island between lines of souvenir stalls.

Corals and dried seaweeds; whelks bubbling in their own juices over charcoal grills; turtle shells and fishing rods, pennants, ray guns, mother of pearl caskets . . . Orville Parr stared about him anxiously as he did his best to shepherd Georgi Nilin and Mikhail hygienically up this narrow, jostling tourist tube. Surges of claustrophobia assaulted him, far worse than on that day at the zoo. He would have to apply for a transfer. He couldn't hold out much longer in this country.

"Why couldn't we arrive by sea?" he whined to Gerry. "The Whale Institute can't possibly get their supplies this way. What is this, an obstacle course?"

Chloe, overhearing him, felt that she knew what the poor man was feeling. The frenzy of those quaysides visibly infected the Japanese holidaymakers. They seemed angry and impatient as they tramped up the cobble path. A jostling indignation, almost indecent haste, showed in the way they seized souvenirs off the stalls, as though those were likely to turn to trash in their hands, and thrust crumpled thousand-yen notes across the counters—money which might fall to cobwebs a moment later . . .

Parr stared at the two drivers, a burly pan-faced couple, squashed into shiny black shoes and shiny Tetoron suits, climbing the tube with the blankly receptive eyes of some fish waiting to gobble indiscreet flies. Their hands hung slackly from their wrists, rigid as boards now they were off the steering wheels.

"Are your chauffeurs armed?" Parr demanded. Fucking two-faced snoopers, he cursed inside himself.

Enozawa thought it was a vulgar query and disdained to answer.

Gerry Mercer saw a black plastic sperm whale and dropped back to buy it. A wrinkled old woman with a bright gold tooth in the center of her mouth dunked it in a bowl of water, held it up and squeezed the sides to show him how it worked. The whale spouted a single jet of water at a forty-five-degree angle. Then she passed the very same dripping toy over with a grin. Jerry held it uncertainly behind his back, not knowing where to put it now. It would soak his coat pocket. He sensed he'd been made a fool of by the woman, subtly.

The stubby white lighthouse at the peak of the island turned out to be a restaurant. Beer crates and soy sauce crates lay piled up outside its door—and an oil drum full to the brim of dying, broken lobsters. The shells had been stripped off their backs for the foamy living flesh to be diced and eaten raw. The husks of the beasts still lived vestigially. Their feelers quested the air slowly for oblivion. What remained of their snapped legs flexed in and out in a parody of motion.

As they filed past they stared down into the drum, the Americans with feelings of queasy alarm at the marine Auschwitz enacted in this trash can, the Japanese with a bland Buddhistic censorship of the notion of pain, Mikhail sheltering the boy from the sight, hauling him up against his body with an immense hand. . . .

From the top of the lava cone here, the view of the bay, distant whaling sheds and gull clouds resumed. That oily whiff was on the air again, intermittently.

To their right sprawled the buildings of the Institute, jutting out into the waters, with—of course! cursed Parr—their own landing stages. There was even a dock with sluice gates big enough to accommodate a full-size baleen whale. Gantries with winches ran out over the dock, extending far back under cover of a huge shed.

Steps cut into the solid lava led down to the institute from the restaurant. Steps led out, too, on to the main lava flow, which fanned out into the bay some way: crimped, bobbled and crinkled as a black lace petticoat. Holidaymakers stood about stagily in various frozen attitudes, clutching cameras, fishing rods, artists' easels, baseball gloves. Occasionally they flickered into activity, pitching a ball, casting a line, or shifting an easel around; then froze once more. The lava was difficult to negotiate smoothly; however, their behavior made every action seem totally disconnected, like a quantum jump.

Sixteen

A motorcycle gang with *SATAN'S SLAVES* painted
on their fuel tanks in phosphorescent glitter had arrived at the barbed-wire fence and was wheeling
about, revving their engines and scattering dust. Tired
soldiers watched them through binoculars from under
the makeshift sunshades they'd run up on top of the
half-tracks, while the off-duty soldiers sprawled dozing on camp beds in the three open-bottomed mar-
quees.

Ruth and Morelli watched them too, sitting in the
Sierra parked on the Mezapico side of the military
vehicles.

Richard had left his binoculars in the glove com-
partment. Morelli used them to read off the Slaves'
name.

"See the worshipers gather, Ruth!" he exclaimed,
with a grim note of vindication—triumph, almost.

Sexuality stirred in Ruth as she stared at the motorcycle gang. She visualized the blond newsman as one
of them, his crew-cut grown long, green forage cap
discarded in favor of a Nazi crash helmet; the scar on

his cheek, result now of a raking with a cycle chain during some rumble of Angels. . . .

But the helicopter that ferried in more soldiers, to match the buildup of pilgrims on the other side, had borne the blond man back to the city with some of the other newsmen.

A series of vivid cartoon stills of him raping her in Angel gear presented itself to her imagination. She closed her eyes to concentrate on the vibrating humiliation of it. The presence of the impotent fiery Italian in the passenger seat beside her enhanced her fantasy. He was so much more *poignant* an escort than Richard Kimble. Gianfranco *knew;* he just *couldn't.* His intense dammed-up energy wound a web of searing mental electricity around her that cocooned her for the time being from Paul's new Promethean countenance. . . .

Relaxing, she reopened her eyes.

Morelli was staring at her intent, pinched, sweat-flushed face with revulsion and fascination.

Suspiciously she sniffed the air. At the height of her fantasy, she could have sworn she'd detected a tang of the blond newsman's shave lotion. . . . Gianfranco was wearing a splash of it. Her barbecue boyfriend had complained about the aerosol can's disappearing from his luggage. So Gianfranco had stolen it? How comical! An inner laugh rocked her, giving her fantasy one last glorious twist. Where that man had been giving off the appropriate male musk for her, however, the Italian seemed to be wearing antiseptic.

Those Satan's Slaves must stink of sweat and grease and marijuana and dried jissom—she was sure!

The Angels wheeled, scattering dust.

The desert resembled a vast inhabited used-car lot, with the hundreds of vehicles parked about at random off the road. Even carts and bicycles. Some shacks had been run up out of cardboard and corrugated iron, scavenged from somewhere. Really they were little more than roofs on poles, but people cooked in them, and sold enchiladas, tortillas, tequila, beer. An air of exhaustion hung over the mass of people. Those who weren't dozing in cars or under trucks were squatting in hunched rows facing the wire and Mount Mezapico beyond as though waiting for a cinema show to start on the blue screen of the sky. . . .

The only people on the move, apart from Angels, were a trible of thirty or forty Californian hippies dancing in slow circles banging tambourines and playing flutes, some in jeans, some in saffron robes. And some isolated individuals wandering about among the scrub and cacti, drunk, drugged, or shocked.

Five thousand people in that shanty encampment, sleeping or sitting in the heat, waiting for nightfall . . .

A priest and two soldiers were down by the wire, extricating a corpse for burial. A row of six crossways-tied sticks already poked up from sand graves.

"I shall file no more reports about *this*," snarled Morelli. "It only makes matters worse. They can give me the sack—"

"Hardly a very dynamic attitude to adopt!" she mocked. "I thought you felt called upon to oppose Paul."

"No one is neutral or immune, I agree. Nobody is simply an observer. But to observe events helps to create them. I do not choose to collaborate in this . . . hysterical new reality."

Switching on the ignition. Ruth rolled the Sierra downhill, past a half-track to the spot where the priest was reading out of a tattered missal. The soldiers leaning on their shovels, their automatic rifles slung across their shoulders, looked more weary than reverent. Morelli climbed out and marched over to the priest. It was the same Father Luis who had rung his bell in protest.

"You're wasting your time, father," he interrupted brutally. "They'll all try to swarm over the wire tonight. The whole mob. They're mesmerized by that light on the mountain. See, it's angled to catch the sun. It's turning slowly to keep the maximum brightness centered in it. That's no observatory. That's a hypnosis machine!"

"Yes," nodded Father Luis. "It is the same as my vision. I foresaw it. It calls them. Bends their minds." He kept his back to Mount Mezapico. "I—will—not —look at it," the old man stammered.

Morelli gripped him by the shoulder with a fierce comradeship.

"Yet, father, have you thought that they might try to *destroy* the machine, if they reach it? Since it is destroying their souls? They need only the idea."

The priest's head rocked in disagreement.

"These . . . are sacrificial goats. It makes no difference. The effect has already . . . ah, spread far beyond them, I hear. Besides, it is not an easy machine to pull down. The soldiers will kill them. . . ."

Leaving the Sierra, too, Ruth strayed nearer the wire. Tatters of cloth hung spiked on it; some barbs were black with flies swarming and resettling. Dried blood.

Circling, a Satan's Slave headed toward her—an unnaturally thin, rangy youth, whose jeans rode high up his dirty leather boots, with the name DANNY picked out in studs on the front of his leather jacket. On the back he'd painted the Devil card from the Tarot pack: the horned God with male and female homunculi chained at its feet. Welded into his helmet were ridiculous, puckish horns—certain to drive right through his skull if he had a bad spill on the highway.

"Hey, Danny," Ruth cooed over the wire.

"Hi, Talent." He jerked a thumb at the charred remnants of the bonfire on his side, and the graves the soldiers were digging on hers. "Like, we miss black mass?"

"Don't worry, there'll be another show tonight. I'd be a big boy and ride on home if I were you."

Danny slapped his machine affectionately across the flank with a bony fist.

"I could bounce this hog over your barbed wire and be up and over the hill before those dumb hick soldiers ever woke up!"

"Don't be too sure of that, Danny Boy."

He stood straddling the bike, preternaturally tall, thin as a rake.

"Say, Talent, lift you over, split a beer with the Slaves, hey?"

"My name's Ruth," she bridled, "not Talent. Ruth *Hammond*."

"Shoot! That right? You his daughter?"

"His wife, Danny."

Danny executed a mock obeisance, stooping over his handlebars till his horns tapped the telescopic front-wheel forks. Whipping upright, he hooted:

"Slaves! I present Hammond's old lady to you! Pick you over the wire, lady, we worship you with our bodies," his long childish face leered.

Ruth leaned, faint, against a wooden crosspiece of the wire, smelling her fantasy come real in the flesh, grease, hair, and leather.

To Danny, it appeared she was bending forward for his arms to lift her over, shutting her eyes like so many chicks surrendering on jerry-built altars behind filling stations, in parking lots. . . .

Dropping his spade across a grave, the nearest Mexican soldier unslung his rifle and waved it at the tall Angel, who grinned back insolently as he reached out to grab this small dark prey, knowing she was between him and any bullet.

Then Morelli sprinted over, spat in the Angel's face, and wrenched Ruth away.

Very slowly, Danny backed his bike.

"My eyes are photographing your features, mister," he shouted. "I advise you memorize them, too! Mrs. Ruth—Satan's Slaves ride for you tonight."

"Piss off," swore Morelli. He shouted at the soldier, in Spanish: "Shoot that scum in the leg—do the world a favor." However the soldier shook his head. It only took a pebble in the pond, to set the ripples spreading. One shot, maybe, to galvanize those thousands of catatonic spectators to a more desperate bout of violence.

Morelli hurried Ruth back up the crumbling slope, gripping her so tightly that the crook of her arm stung.

Would Richard Kimble have dragged her out of bed
with that newsman as fiercely because he disap-
proved? No. Richard had stood there gawping and
whining. The Italian was potent in his darkest impotence.

"Filthy West Coast degenerates," he raged. "What
did you think you were doing, Ruth? Cockteasing
them? While your husband hypnotizes the whole
world, is this the best you can imagine for yourself?"

"I felt faint down there," she excused herself. "So
many people, and they're all Paul's doing—it horrifies
me. The phony bastard . . ."

"Would you say so out loud in public, Ruth?"

"Uh?"

"Will you help me?"

"To pull Paul down?" She shook her head morose-
ly. "He's for real. Authentic. A genius. You know
Rasputin? They shot him, poisoned him and drowned
him, yet still he walked and talked and mesmerized
people. They couldn't finish him off with axes, those
quilted Russian coats they wear. I've been reading
about him in *The Reader's Digest*. Rasputin was only
a country magician. Paul's a great scientist—he doesn't
need crystal balls. He has a radiotelescope, the biggest
looking-glass in all history! He has a galaxy called
after him . . . Rasputin was a pig with women," she
rambled on, "and they adored him. Paul seems pretty
cool and suave that way. Did you know he's really
awful in bed?"

Morelli's eyes clouded.

Ruth's expression was twisted midway between the
axes of laughter and commiseration.

"He can do it," she emphasized, "he's just lousy as a
lover. Damn him, he thinks he's as brilliant at sex as
at everything else!"

"Have you told him to his face he's no good in bed,
Ruth?"

She shook her head.

"Do it," he whispered fiercely. "For God's sake, do
it!"

"Maybe it's me that's lousy, not him. He'd divorce

me—it wouldn't pull the carpet out from under him—"

"Sexual performance is very near the kernel of a man's ego," Morelli forced himself to say. "Sexual despair is the most devastating despair."

"Despair of existence itself is worse," chided Father Luis.

"One can lead straight on to the other! A man's being is a sexual thing. All his works are sublimations."

"You overvalue it," the old priest said gently.

"Hammond's theory of nothingness is surely a projection of his own hidden fears onto the greatest screen he has available."

"My son, the whole world is sick with nothingness. But it does not fear a failure of sexuality. It fears starvation, it fears too many people through the agency of sexuality. The decay of civilization, the vanishing of fuel, the poisoning of the seas—these it fears!" His flimsy hand gestured at the Pacific, visible as a vivid blue streak along the desert edge.

"The seas? Our greatest sexual symbol!" raved Morelli. "*Thalassa,* the Sea, is the womb of our being. Once we poison that, we sterilize ourselves. As the fish die, so we kill the sperm of the spirit!"

Ruth drew fractionally away from him, closer to the soldiers. He seemed distraught enough to attack her. She had no wish to be mutilated, like him.

(Yet only moments earlier she dreamed of a rape by Angels? Would that have left her untarnished? Or with tribal marks razored in her cheeks? Branded on her breasts!)

"Sex is the life energy, but we have used up the whole planet's energy, and without energy we are impotent. In our hearts we know this, father, so we seek a religion of impotence—that the universe may reflect ourselves. What we seek, we shall surely find, for the most scientific of reasons!"

The Land Rover that Morelli had formerly arrived in rounded the bend in the road from San Pedro, then, with Richard Kimble at the wheel and Paul Hammond in the passenger seat ...

The spectacle of Hammond actually coming in person to inspect this flimsy boundary of hysteria he had created horrified Morelli into silence. With anyone else it would have been sheer irresponsibility. But is the megalomaniac "irresponsible"? On the contrary, his is a case of aggravated responsibility. We speak of diminished responsibility. So why not aggravated responsibility? He makes himself responsible for everything.

"I thought you might be in danger here, Ruth," boomed Hammond as he clambered out, while Kimble kept the engine idling. "Fool, Morelli, bringing her here!"

"Far stupider, *you* coming here!"

"I have to protect my wife. Obviously you have no sense. Climb in with me, Ruth, and Richard can drive the Sierra back." He made no mention of giving Morelli a lift—in his own hired vehicle.

Ruth thought Paul was going to take her by the arm as Morelli had a moment before, but her husband walked right past her and down to the wire barricade where he halted and stared across. A Mexican lieutenant ran from one of the tents and began begging him to leave. Impatiently, Hammond yawned.

Far away on Mezapico Mountain, the Big Dish held a spoonful of condensed sunlight, burning it into the retinas of the crowd . . .

Angel Danny coasted his bike back to the wire and stared at Dr. Paul.

Then whooped his name aloud.

Rashly, the lieutenant jerked his pistol from its holster. Waving it at the bike's front wheel, he squeezed the trigger. Paul Hammond neatly seized hold of the officer's elbow and jerked it—but to re-aim the gun, not drag it aside. Richard Kimble could see that much quite plainly from where he was sitting. Magnified at the end of a visual tunnel: the hand. The gun. The accurate aim.

The bullet struck the fuel tank instead of the wheel, and the tank exploded in a ball of fire. Flames snaked up the lanky, rearing figure of the Angel, spattering a few gobs across the wire. Hammond danced back nimbly, leaving the lieutenant to be slightly scalded by burning petrol. The officer dropped his pistol with a yelp and fled back toward the tents, shouting.

Danny fell screaming over and over in the sand. The painted devil on his back darted out particularly bright green tongues of flames. He finally lay extinguished twenty yards from his burning machine, legs kicking spasmodically like a giant electrified frog's. . . .

Yet the other Slaves had heard what he shouted out. Chanting the name "Hammond!" in chorus, they gunned their bikes towards their leader's body. And the name sped back among the crouched ranks facing the mountain. With the undulant motion of a millipede, the crowd rose and wavered.

Hammond propelled Ruth bodily towards the Land Rover, ignoring her protests.

"Get out, Richard! Drive the Sierra!"

Kimble sat stubbornly still.

"You killed him, Paul. I saw you point the gun—"

"He's not dead, just hurt—they're pulling him to his feet—see? Walking him away—"

"Dragging him, he's dying—"

"Damn you, Richard, will you get out! Or we'll all be dead—"

Ignoring the shooting entirely, as though it was an irrelevance, Morelli demanded:

"Why is your telescope always reflecting the sun this way, Dr. Hammond?"

"What the hell are you talking about? The dish follows an automatic program. It's locked onto one of the microwave discrepancies. I haven't time for interviews now."

"It's locked on to us, down here."

Hammond forced the Italian away with a brisk punch in the chest, and pulled open the passenger door to bundle Ruth inside. She huddled there miserably, while he marched round the vehicle and wrenched Richard's door open.

Richard was still sitting there, refusing to make a move, when a light machine-gun opened fire from the top of the nearest half-track, kicking up a line of dust along the near side of the wire.

A susurrus of sound rippled among the crowd: wind over human wheat . . .

Richard scrambled out smartly and raced for the Sierra.

"Hurry up Morelli," he called over his shoulder. "Come with me!"

The Italian was perfectly right about the telescope, he realized.

The machine gun raked the wire again, ripping dusty pockmarks.

Seventeen

Bob Pasko had outlined the problem to Dr. Kato. Behind those rimless bifocals, hooded eyes were already squinting at the matter inwardly. The old man's field of vision might terminate a few meters in front of him; but it stretched back to a remote vanishing point far inside his head.

Kato was also thinking pleasurable thoughts of seeing Miss Patton again. Her dumpiness tickled him erotically. She possessed the lavish stumpiness of a fat-calfed peasant maid in a resort inn, kneeling in tight bright kimono offering a saké flask to a tipsy old man and playing in the bath with him. Visitors to his office were served weak green tea by such a girl, recruited from the countryside, wearing a nurse's white coat.

Enozawa talked rapidly to the old man in tight bursts of Japanese. The breathless strangleholds on the even flow of his speech implied a certain deference; however it was a staccato, impatient deference, and even the polite verbal tentatives that Enozawa used snapped off short, like broken lobster feelers.

Kato inspected Georgi Nilin curiously while Enozawa was speaking—nodding meanwhile at most of the
pauses, slipping in verbal punctuation in counterpoint
. . . "hai! . . . ee . . . so . . ."

The child coolly returned his gaze. He even sipped
the brackish green tea, scorning the candy bar Pasko
had produced from his pocket.

"I did think of that, Mr. Pasko," Kato laughed
gently, as the psychiatrist tossed the candy in the
trash can irritably. "But I reasoned that a porcelain
cup of Japanese tea might be a better test of his adult-
hood as opposed to his childishness, you see?"

Setting his cup down with great precision on Kato's
desk, the boy slid off his seat to pursue his relentless
quest for paper clips and rubber bands and pencils
and other office paraphernalia, which his fingers began
knitting obsessively into an assemblage. A pseudo-ma-
chine took form on the desk, then, ungainly and precarious. But it held together.

Meanwhile, while he assembled this machine, they
discussed his own assembly. . . .

"They must have imprinted different aspects of the
mind model on his brain at different periods," the psychiatrist suggested thoughtfully. "Alternatively, the
total model many times over. The infant brain simply
doesn't mature at an even rate, and you can't program
when the circuitry isn't available. Why, we're still not
sure whether many of the neurons are capable of
transmitting impulses at all for ages. The myelin insulation's still being laid down along the axons for at
least the first two years of life, hand in glove with
the kid's behavioral development."

"Ah, but which comes first?" interrupted Tom Winterburn. "Does traffic along the nerves trigger the insulation effect? Or is it insulation that makes traffic
possible? If it's the first, then interference by imprinting
could actually set up pathways—in other words *force*
development: speed up pathway formation. But I
agree this consciousness transplant isn't likely to be
produced straight off. Personally I think it must be by

reinforcement, using the total model, over a long period. But how long a period?"

"You're assuming the boy *is* programmed? I'm only
theorizing, you know."

"I've got to assume it, don't you see? If they're using
the 370-185 on Sakhalin to program human personality
models into sperm whales and lord knows what else!"
Tom Winterburn turned to Kato. "Well, sir, do you
think it is possible?"

"We brought him here, too," babbled Orville Parr
rudely, his claustrophobic anxieties unabated, "in case
anything triggers him, the way the zoo did. Pasko's
told you about that? And the kid seems to like communicating through models. Objects, not words—"

"We have many models of whale brains here,"
blinked Kato. "Sections of genuine brains, too. Our
agents on the whaling boats collect these, whenever
feasible. We have a number of *handô iruka* too . . . dolphins, embalmed alive, not to mention a small *shachi*, a killer-whale baby. . . ." He smiled, with polite
connoisseurship.

"Embalmed *alive?*" Chloe fluttered.

"Vital perfusion technique, Chloe!" Herb Flynn
hissed. "It's standard practice. The anesthetized animal
has its blood replaced by a saline solution, then by preservative. Technically it's alive. Not conscious, of
course. It can never recover consciousness. But we can
still run some electrode stimulus tests on the brain."

"Oh, yes. Of course." She nodded, lamely. "Vital
perfusion" sounded like such a life-giving phrase, like
"blood transfusion." "Embalming alive" gave off a mus-
ty stench.

"Miss Patton's basically on the training side," Flynn
remarked disparagingly. "Swimming pools. Fun and
games."

"Quite," laughed Kato. "Miss Patton and I are old
friends, *né?*" He gazed at her plump body dreamily,
fitting it into a bright flowery kimono.

Sensing an awkwardness in the situation, Gerry
Mercer gallantly produced the plastic toy he'd bought
from behind his back.

"Say, speaking of models, I picked this up on the way."

"Ah, our old friend the *makkô kujira*," giggled Kato, in an access of childish hilarity. "The suspect." Tears came to his eyes, behind the owlish glasses, at the spectacle of such a toy being seriously flourished inside his institute. Herb Flynn directed a withering glare at Mercer, who blushed furiously; nevertheless he still stepped forward to offer Georgi Nilin the toy.

The boy uttered a cry and clutched at it.

Vindicated, grinning broadly, Gerry handed the whale over.

But it still had some water in it, unfortunately. As soon as the boy squeezed the whale's sides it spouted, sprinkling Dr. Kato with spray.

"I'm sorry, sir!" Gerry rushed forward with a handkerchief.

Kato removed his spectacles and very delicately wiped them dry, using his own handkerchief.

"Boys will be boys," he remarked. But who was the boy—Georgi or Gerry? Hard to say.

"Perhaps you'd be kind enough to show us around, sir?" Pasko suggested, more diplomatically. "As Mr. Parr says, something may trigger Nilin."

"*Da, da, da,*" the boy chanted, wagging the black plastic whale at the machine he'd assembled on Kato's desk. "*Kit, kit! Kachalot kit!*"

The boy clutched his new toy fiercely as Mikhail led him out, at a gesture from Dr. Kato.

"Young Georgi's using that word 'kit' in both senses; I'll swear to it," muttered Tom Winterburn. "The intonation's different. Whale, in Russian. Construction set, in English. The whale is a . . ."

"Construction set," nodded Pasko. "And vice versa. Maybe."

Tom Winterburn shook his head.

"No, I think it's more complicated than that."

Herb Flynn indicated the dolphin brain model to Chloe Patton impatiently: a three-dimensional jig-saw puzzle composed of variously colored transparent plastic segments, the whole assemblage being enclosed inside a colorless cylinder contoured to represent a section of the animal's head. A realistic blowhole cut one channel down through it, to the rear of the brain. In front of the blowhole, a second larger tunnel had been carved down through the plastic representing muscle tissue, to lay bare a dime-sized patch of "skull", in which a neat hole was drilled.

"That's how we do it at San Diego, too. Recall, Chloe?" Herb stuck his finger down the second tunnel briefly, then raked his fingernail across the plastic case, ticking off the name tags stenciled inside the model one by one, while Kato looked on benignly.

"Cerebrum up here. . . . Medulla right at the base. The insulating tube for the electrode goes right down through the brain tissue as far as the top of the cerebellum, here, see? Then you feed the electrode through it. Understand, Chloe? This area is the brain's control board for voluntary movements. So we can test our motor functions by stimulating it—"

"Yes," whispered Chloe distractedly, willing him to move on to the brain models of larger whales, which were less emotive for her.

"Interesting, né, the cerebellum?" Kato restrained her with a pluck at her plump arm. "It follows the standard mammalian scheme—yet with so many unusual features of its own! The vast size of the paraflocculus, here, né? Then the extreme shrinkage of the flocculo-nodular lobe. But these relate to control of the body shape in swimming, so you might expect it. All this area would have to be left undisturbed—'on automatic pilot' as you say—in any mind transfer. And the same applies to our friend the makkô kujira."

He led her onward at last, with another pinch of her flesh, toward the next plastic brain: a far larger model labeled in Latin Physeter catodon.

"The sperm whale, so. This brain weighs almost nine kilos. Absolute weight means nothing, né? Or the elephant would be a philosopher. Yet if we compare the brain-stem ratios of man and makkô, or match the complexity of the cerebrum, makkô seems to be our equal! Privately, I think it is nonsense to imagine *makkô* as 'intelligent' in our human sense. Still, with this degree of complexity, and given this bulk of brain matter, some human intelligence can be printed on to it, perhaps? Look, the cerebral cortex is so extremely convoluted, is it not The seat of consciousness. . . . Here is where any such printing must occur, I think. . . ."

He faced Tom Winterburn, keeping Chloe Patton's arm firmly secured.

"You ask is it possible?" he sighed. "Ah, such discrepancies between human brain and whale brain! See, a premotor area occupies much of the frontal lobes. In men the area handles conscious planning and foresight. I suspect this may control all the tubes in the whale's brow. I believe 'melon' is the English name. But what has that got to do with intelligent planning? Nothing. So for me this proves a lack of human-style intellect in the whale. Also, the whale's frontal lobe lacks any association area—another discrepancy! On the other hand, the toothed whales certainly have no sense of smell, so we should expect to find the olfactory center missing. The hippocampus and mammillary body are absent, yes, but see, here are the amygdaloid nucleus and olfactory tubercle! They are present. Why? What role do they play? Who knows? The Russians?"

He ran his free hand along the length of the model.

"See how compressed the whale brain is from front to back, *né*? The whole brain is telescoped and twisted. A question of skull structure. How can we hope to superimpose a map of the human mind onto *this*? The locations are all displaced and warped."

"Excuse me, sir, but I feel we're being led astray by your sort of models," Tom Winterburn broke in. "Sure, they're beautifully made. But I say they're misleading in this instance."

Bob Pasko groaned inwardly. Kato had devoted only his whole life to producing them! Thank God that dumpy bobby-soxer was here to titillate the old man. . . . He saw the logic of her presence now. At least

someone, somewhere—in San Diego presumably—had
an idea how to handle people.

"Your models, sir, suggest taking something apart
and putting it together again, in whole units like a jig-
saw puzzle. Swapping parts of a kit around—"

Georgi, who'd been gazing intently at the colored
plastic brain all the while, emitted a tiny cry at the
sound of the word . . .

"What I'm thinking about is a *mathematical* model,
that can be stored and remodeled mathematically to fit
a new shape, without necessarily disturbing the content. A few simplified mathematical models of human
brain activity are already available in the West. The
370–185 could eat those for breakfast. And, speaking
of maps, sir, did you know there's a math technique
called 'mapping' that has nothing to do with drawing
representational diagrams? It's part of Hilbertian
mathematics—a way of translating abstract models
from one mode into another. Geometrical designs may
look very different but they can be 'mapped' algebraically and shown to have the same abstract structure. Why not do something of the sort with abstract
models of different kinds of brain?"

Kato shrugged, offended.

"I'm not a mathematician. I am a biologist. Time to
look at the embalming tanks, I think." He nipped
Chloe Patton hard enough to make her yelp. She
vividly remembered those pictures of curvy girls in the
sadomasochistic comics on the quayside stalls.

"I don't want to see embalming tanks," she pouted.

"But we have a small *shachi*, my dear. There is also
a baby *makkô kujira* we obtained from the womb, on
the point of birth!"

So they had a sperm whale here, in the flesh! Pasko
thought hastily. Kato had clearly been saving this item
up till last. Obviously it was crucial for Georgi to see
the whale.

Go on, Chloe! he willed, realizing how Kato might
refuse in pique, if Miss Patton misbehaved, this coming straight upon Tom Winterburn's derogatory remarks. Wishing fervently that telepathy existed and

trying to convey it all by facial language alone, Bob Pasko smiled urgent encouragement. Go and see his lousy embalming tanks, even if they remind you of those lobster husks outside the café. Grab the electrode chopsticks and dig in to the meat! Accept a pinch on the ass, too!

"Okay," nodded Chloe after a moment's thought, "let's see your baby sperm whale. For little Georgi's sake," she added, meeting Pasko's eyes with a pained expression.

Full marks, Chloe! the psychiatrist breathed.

Eighteen

The unborn sperm whale floating in preservative was four meters long. Its skull had been sectioned open to reveal the naked brain, and its melon drained of spermaceti, leaving the brow cavity a hopeless tangle of collapsed entraillike tubing. The slim plate of the lower jaw hung slackly open—an upside-down lid for the great tub of the upper jaw. . . .

Georgi Nilin cried out as soon as he saw the tank, broke free from the *muzhik*'s side and ran to it, gesticulating.

"*Daitye radio! Viklyuchitye!*"

"He wants a radio set," Tom Winterburn translated, puzzled. Chloe Patton hurriedly volunteered to go and fetch one, though she hadn't the slightest idea where one was to be found.

"A chauffeur will do that sort of thing," Kato said peevishly. Duly instructed, one of Enozawa's drivers trotted off, leather soles clicking into the distance.

"Autists feel safer with machines," Pasko commented tactfully. "If he's just an autist! Predictable responses, you know. On, it's on. Off, it's off—"

127

"Maybe he wants to repair the beast's head, symbolically?" Flynn suggested. "Possibly he wants that 'kit' he put together in Dr. Kato's room? Maybe that's his radio?"

"Shall I fetch it just in case?" Chloe's body wavered toward the exit.

"No," Pasko said brusquely. "I mean, yes, but I'll fetch it, Miss Patton. I watched how the kid put it together so I know where the weak points are. I'm collecting those models of his, to study."

"The other chauffeur," remarked Enozawa, "is a very dainty man. In his spare time he dwarfs trees. He won't break your toy."

Pasko shrugged. It didn't much matter to him whether the driver broke the thing or not, so long as Chloe Patton stayed put. So the other chauffeur trotted off, too—at a mere nod from Captain Enozawa, Orville Parr observed. Not even keeping up the pretense of telling the man what to do in Japanese, this time! Oh, yes, they spoke English, all right. They listened to everything. Just as that Nikon camera filmed him, in his own office, over the rooftops!

Then the first driver came back with a transistor set and Pasko presented it to Georgi Nilin. Instantly the boy was tugging and clamoring to be hoisted up level with the top of the tank. Once there, he directed his *muzhik* calmly with swimming notions of his body till he hung poised in space above the cut-away brain.

The boy switched the radio on.

A surge of orchestral music filled the hall.

"Beethoven's *Pastoral*," Kato identified. Chloe Patton couldn't imagine any music less suitable to the chilly preserving chamber than this golden-grained surge of sounds.

Georgi flipped forward in a nosedive, and would have plunged right into the fluid if hands less burly than Mikhail's had been gripping him. As it was, he stuck his arms into the liquid up to his elbows, and carefully balanced the radio on the whale's broad neck, just to the rear of where it had been sliced open.

The radio carried on playing, submerged, though

what had been a golden surge became a sullen, mooing boom.

"Sounds like a whale song now, all right!" laughed
Flynn.

"But not a sperm-whale song, Herb! That's the one
whale it doesn't sound like. Sperm whales only click,
like Geiger counters. That's all they do. Clicking. No
singing."

"Kik," chanted Georgi. "Ki-ki-ki-kik!"

"Well, he agrees with you, Tom."

"You're not *thinking*, Herb! Just supposing it was
any other whale they'd used. The Russians could
hear its actual voice hundreds of miles away underwater, couldn't they?"

The hairy, acne-welted face assented.

"If it was a humpback, and if it got in between two
reflecting layers, and put out a hundred decibels, it's
detectable up to—oh, twenty-five thousand miles
away, theoretically—"

"Come again?" exclaimed Parr incredulously.

"I said twenty-five thousand miles, under perfect
conditions."

"Christ. You've run out of sea by then—"

"Or gone right around the globe!" grinned Herb
Flynn. "It's a curved universe for whales, Mr. Parr.
They shouldn't have as much trouble with Einsteinian
space as we do!"

Pasko noticed a nervous twitch in Kato's left eye,
at the mention of Einstein and space. . . . And the old
man had relinquished Chloe Patton's arm, too. She
took prompt advantage of her liberation to scurry
around the tank to the other side, pretending an intense interest in something there.

The second driver had trotted back, by now, with
Georgi's "machine"; but nobody seemed interested in
it now, least of all the boy, whose gaze was locked
firmly on the transistor radio still mooing on the whale's
neck. The Japanese stood holding the construction,
delicately, between his wooden hands.

"How far do sperm-whale clicks travel, Herb?"

"Six or seven miles, Tom, that's all."

"So they'd have to communicate with their sperm whale by radio. Which means one must be surgically implanted in its head!"

"What do they use for signals? Morse code? Sperm-whale clicks sound like some sort of Morse." It was a flippant suggestion; however Tom Winterburn took it seriously.

"Doubt it. You're assuming there's a Russian-speaking 'pilot' operating the whale. That's half the trouble with these plastic models of Kato's. They make you visualize the wrong thing. Problem: how to insert a Russian radio operator? Remove Part A from the whale kit and substitute a corresponding part from your human kit? Oh, no! The whale brain simply isn't built *overall* to process human language. Even human language in Morse code form. It's still the same language, after all. Human-talk. Some kind of symbolic code would have to be devised that's compatible with the way the whale processes its own signals. You can't just imprint a whale with a knowledge of Russian. You might get away with imprinting a fellow human being. We already have a plan for acquiring human languages wired into us. But another species hasn't. This is a goddamn puzzle! Human language and consciousness are so tightly bound up. I don't see how you can have the second without the first—" He stroked his nose thoughtfully. All his features were azure in this light: a frozen polar explorer's.

"You must admit it would be far simpler training a whale using electrodes in the pain and pleasure centers, now wouldn't it, Tom? You're sure we aren't hunting a red herring?" Flynn cackled briefly. "Or a red whale?"

Orville Parr nodded vigorous assent; however the polar figure still insisted:

"It all depends on what you want your whale to do. If you just want it to dive-bomb submarines automatically, okay, I go along with you. If you want it to spy for you and communicate *with* you, somehow you've got to map 'humanity' into the beast. But how on earth can you pack all the information you'd need, into coded radio signals a few clicks long?"

"Chloe Patton popped up briefly from behind the tank.

"It's unfair calling the sperm-whale noises 'clicks', Captain Winterburn. Think of the birds. We hear a single chirrup in the garden, but that chirrup's made up of a hundred separate sounds at least. And the bird can distinguish them all."

"Hang on, Miss Patton. How many separate sounds would you say there are in a whale click?"

"Oh, I've seen oscilloscope photos with dozens of pulses packed into twenty *microseconds*."

"So what we hear as a single click could carry a complicated message? In symbolic code?"

"Somebody's done some work on this." Herb Flynn burrowed irritably in his briefcase. "Rather eccentric speculations, if I remember. Still, I brought it along. Yes, here we are. About decoding *Physeter* signals and using their code for . . . God yes, this is the crazy bit. He's an astronomer; he suggests using whale clicks for coding cosmic messages. The *Review of Biological Psychology* printed it. That's eccentrics' forum. Still, since we're in the zany ideas lobby anyway, with a humanoid whale. . . ." He broke off, staring at the offprint in his hand. "Sweet Christ! The man who wrote this is on Paul Hammond's staff. Talk about a madness bug!"

Kato was sweating faintly now—like the glass of his preserving tank, with so many people breathing on it.

"I have to know," the Japanese biologist cut in harshly. "That man's ideas—do they represent a scientific consensus? The *kami no ashioto, né*? I have tried so hard not to think about it."

"The Footfalls of God," Enozawa translated crisply, his voice tight as a salute.

"Yes, the nothingness at the core," the old man murmured. "It seems to be the *seppuku* of the Western soul." He drew his thumb expressively from left to right across his midriff, ending the gesture with a sharp upward twist—turning the key off in the human machine. "Of science, too? We might all be happier to *know* there is nothing, and that we are nothing. We Japanese have ruined our countryside for the sake of doing like the West. Now there are too many of us to slacken pace. We must march on, but not into light —into darkness!"

Enozawa stiffened resolutely. To hear the old director talking of *seppuku,* calling the deed by its honorific name, instead of the vulgar *hara-kiri,* how it heartened him! Old values could still be restored.

"How strange," meditated Kato, "that American science should commit this act of nihilism. That those who landed on the moon should now look as far as the eye can see, and say 'There is nothing.' We Japanese have always felt very close to nothingness. Our economy is the great contradiction of this inner sense. We can hardly understand the paradox ourselves. Now it all comes to an end. Do you know what we are really doing in this institute? Conducting an autopsy. Fish, whales . . . We shall soon be starving in these islands. And we are not even permitted to catch sperm whales any more. But there is no intelligent whale, I tell you . . . I do not believe it! Yet we have to starve because you Americans believe it." He stared hard at Chloe Patton, as though her excess fat were blubber filched from Japanese whales, and Japanese mouths; then blinked down at his own body through the bottom half of his bifocals. "Every atom of this body . . . nonbeing . . . soon."

Pathetically, the director gazed over the tank at Chloe Patton's plumpness again; this time, as though to reassure himself of her solidity, forgiving her for the sake of that. Chloe continued to evade his gaze.

"Say, how about us stealing one of Hammond's aces off him? We could commandeer this bright boy of his, hmm?" Orville Parr's voice was a pasty squeak: a lump of putty, dragged along wet glass.

But they agreed with him.

Enozawa walked into Parr's office two days later, while Parr was watching the taxis flying through the haze in their usual panic storm. They'd be the last to go. When they stopped, Tokyo died. . . . They should drive off the expressway parapets to a thousand fire deaths, instead! And Enozawa in one of them.

"Dr. Kato committed suicide last night," the Japanese stated primly, as Parr swiveled around. "We believe there is an onus—an obligation on yourselves and on America for this event. Dr. Kato was one of those whose research might have helped feed us. Consequently, in the matter of Nilin—"

"Don't worry, that'll all be tied up in a couple days more," Parr soothed. "I promise you. We're flying out this whale-click specialist from Mexico. . . . Say, I'm sorry about Dr. Kato, I mean sincerely sorry. It's shocking news. I'm . . . taken aback. I can't register it yet—it's awful." He hesitated, but curiosity overcame discretion. "How did he . . . ? It is rude to ask?"

"Dr. Kato destroyed his models with a fire ax and then smashed the preserving tanks. He cut his wrists with the broken glass. He died of shock and bleeding in hospital."

It had hurt; it had taken courage, thought Enozawa. Yet it hadn't been calm. Director Kato had failed to prepare his spirit. He went on an old man's rampage, almost an act of petulance.

But Parr was remembering Gerry's squirting the old fellow with water, Tom Winterburn's discrediting his brain models—and that Chloe Patton playing hard to get. The Japanese naturally regarded them as responsible. . . . And while he remembered, and wished he was somewhere else, his eyes flickered helplessly back to the morning papers.

MEX RIOT THREAT TO BIG DISH: 130 SAID DEAD
blared the *Pacific Stars and Stripes.*

SUICIDE PLAGUE HITS U.S.: RAPES, HOMOCIDES SOAR
blazoned the English-language *Mainichi Daily News.*

Nineteen

His flipper aches from the chomp of the bull's jaws, but it isn't seriously damaged. He swims obediently now, while the bull dawdles far behind him, sending out only occasional pulses to track him.

An expectant silence stills the ocean, which the bull seems chary of disturbing.

The Big Wailing Ones—those gossips of the sea—have been hushed by the leaping, dancing Click-Whistlers, those who can send two modes of signal together: and because they can send two modes, those were the first (as sheer game, to start with) to leap the gap between clicks of his Own Kind, and whistles of the Singers. Songs so vast that they can cross whole seas. . . .

As he swims, he thinks of what the bull has pulsed to him. . . .

Tens of centuries to attune the Wailing Ones! His Own Kind can pulse out songs direct to them now. But the leaping little Click-Whistlers still do it faster. Such vivid, playful, speedy Ones! They toy with ideas as with floating wood or weedmass—butting and nodding notions about brightly in the kaleidoscopes of their minds. Alas, they cannot fix ideas in glyphs. Their kaleidoscopes keep turning, losing the bright patterns of their thoughts in play.

However long they whistle the signatures of the great glyphs, they can only turn them through an axis or two, in whistletalk. New glyphs are beyond them, till his Own Kind state them.

If they weren't so happy, this might be their tragedy. They sense so much more than the Dumb Wailing Ones, of the inner order of a glyph. Guess at that deep moment of the Star, when a glyph becomes a map of thought, image of the world: when his Own Kind swim mind in mind, dreaming down the sea years through simpler and simpler glyphs of understanding as the aeons drop away, back to the simplest, First glyph of all in the melting midst of an Ice Age . . .

By comparison, his Own Kind's evolution to awareness is a tangible planned thing, mapped in the glyph stages in their brows. They can almost direct that evolution now, by choice of glyph refinements—molding the melon through choice of sounds, in star-glyph after star-glyph, toward megaglyphs of awareness still far away down the swimming ages, still unattainable, yet guessed at as The Goal.

A process slow as the growing of a coral atoll—to enclose a pool of water, reflecting exact images clarified out of the wave tumble of Time, and Being.

The Stars will build this mirror, cell by cell, in soft honeycomb brows.

While the Click-Whistlers wonder at this enterprise, and caper around it, playing games. Sad that they can't enter a Star, with their tiny bodies and brows—when they are the ones who linked the glyphs to the songs of the Crying Ones, so that new glyphs can be known throughout the seas. Yet not so sad for them, as they gambol and copulate and whistle, leaping and dancing on their tails. . . .

He pulses a chary click; hears Three, and then another Three, converging on the same point of ocean. Six points of the Star. He is Seven.

He meets them nose to nose: old male, old female, younger female in one Threesome; three strong bulls in the other.

Slack, calm day—easy to stay in position, waving flukes. Almost as easy as holding (hands)!

His left eye glimpses flank and eye of the oldest bull; his right eye squints at the old female. Of the others, he sees nothing at all—only feels the butt of their brows, as they rock in and out.

"We repeat a simple Glyph," the oldest bull burst-pulses, "CONGRUENCE. Tune our seven clicks to CONGRUENCE. CONGRUENCE opens the mouth to the Greater Glyphs—"

In the mobile wax, a ghostly, dissolving diagram conjures out of sound. The wax, at sea level, being still in its most fluid, oily state. Pulsing a repeat of it, he reads the same image printed briefly on six other melons. . . .

Ranged in the Star, there's only inward to be heard from, only the oily sculptures conjured by their voices to hear. No more world of sea and sweetmeats. Bodies block off all outside sounds, in seven directions. Seven melons are the sole field of attention.

Pulsing, the ghost gathers strength; and interlocks in a sevenfold chain of wax—an annular polygon. . . .

Thoughts cluster round the glyph. . . . Thoughts articulated, in waxen crystals.

CONGRUENCE is a (key), he reasons. What's a (key)?

A (hand) turns a (key). The (key) almost always locks; rarely opens . . . The (hand) then, is congruent with a lock. Five bars curl around in a cage, to make a (hand). One short bar. And four long bars. Bending. Locking.

This cage fits onto things. It acts on things. Things obey it. Thus things are made—such as (steels).

But the (hand)-cage is flexible too, caressing hair,

the lips, the penis. It even opens up flat and seems not
to be a cage at times. Yet it is only the model of a
cage, unfolded. Thus it makes fools of us. (But who is
"us"?) For it seems so open and free, so extensive, always reaching out. We pity those who lack these flat,
soft cages. The Cageless Ones, we think of them as.
They have no grasp of situations. No grip on the
world.

(But who is "WE"!! Who is "WE"!!)

This (hand) has formed the mind, the thoughts,
the (words.) Minds, thoughts and (words) have all
followed the contours of (hand), unwittingly. How
could I be aware of this, when awareness is of the
same shape as what it should be aware of? One fits the
other perfectly, so that one never notices this . . .
Awareness takes (hand's) five and tens for numbers.
Accepts its grip on things for relations in the world.
(Hand) closes around awareness in a cage—and
so subtly is it done that cage and awareness appear
identical, and call themselves Consciousness. . . .

"What are those (Hands), (Words)?"

The question is his own.

It's theirs, too.

For they are congruent, the Seven. The Glyph
prints itself in their brow oil, fades, reprints itself. . . .
In the congruent intervals, questions take form. . . .

"(Hands)? (Words)?" Probing. Insisting. Con-
structing an image of him, around the Glyph. Filling
in gaps in his own self-image, till his mind floats
physically, mapped in oil . . . The resonating Glyph
teases it out and frames it. The liquid mirror hints. . . .

"There is Another One, in him—"

"The faintness of another being—"

"What are these (hands), (words), (steels)?"

"The Glyph can be tuned. Dilated. More is implied—"

"Star can tune this other being—"

"Are you reluctant?"

"To know who I am?" he replied. "How can I be?"

Soon, a sharpening of the self-image . . .

"You are an (instrument), a (tool)—"

"The relation between your two Selves was carved by (Steel)—"

"Yet there was love in your making, too. Do you know this love?"

"Love . . . yes. There was snow, there were (trees)! Yet I saw nothing through my eyes. I had to be led by the (hand). . . . She led me. She she she. Thin, tiny. How could she lead my bulk?"

"The other being in you—"

"We can tune this Being more—"

"A point here, a point there: separated sparks of the Reality—"

"Dots of a glyph of Being—"

"We link them in a net. A web emerges. The self that hides—"

"Let's us repeat a higher Glyph, REPRESENTER—"

Sound booms through their brows then. A new sound is echoed, reechoed. Magnified resonances print the oil till a new Glyph of complex wax transects them —their oil stiffening as though they're deep under tons of sea, diving to the deep floor. . . .

While the wax remains hard, a sound ghost vibrates into being again. Bits of a lattice built for another reason regain their old, lost order. A ghost surfaces through his invented being and floats in the wax annulus, within the Seven.

Awareness of himself hangs brief as a jellyfish dissolving on the shore; melts as the wax melts back to oil.

The Seven suck air, blow foam across each other's backs . . . and regard the image of him in their memories.

He's exhausted by the strain of sustaining that density of wax, which should weigh him down on a dive. But amazed.

"We must form the Star again, together. You are only a pup; need resting and feeding, strength to sustain the Star. We held the Glyph up for you in your brow, then. Condition of dependency."

"You are used to making sounds with (Steels). With (Steel Instruments). Strange. Let us rethink the map of you that was spun around REPRESENTER—"

"You will learn to carry this Glyph," clicks the old female, more kindly. "Even the Great Glyphs RESONATOR, CONCEIVER, TRANSCENDER . . . But you must go now. For a while. Till we think how to cure you. Hear this—

"Once, World was a single point of sound, in a womb woven of silence. Time passed, and the first sound echoed and reechoed, till it became many sounds. World was woven from waves of sound crossing, vibrating, for a million ages. Till sounds stiffened into the hard wax of the world, with all its shapes of Being, and the soft wax of the sea. All is born of sound. Yet not by this thing (Word), be sure! (Word) and (Hand) are destroyers of sound. Disrupters. They rupture the womb of silence itself . . . We must pulse a song for the Wailing Ones to warn Our Kind. Nothing may warp the searoad of the Glyphs . . . Oh so slowly we have followed it, ever since the mid-Time of Ice!"

Twenty

"He's taken part in the Thought Complex!" Katya cried exultantly, bursting in on Kapelka, waving the latest printout.

"Katerina Afanasyevna!" the professor chided her, using the formal mode of address for the first time in many months. He indicated the other occupant of the room: a bulky man draped in a thick black fur coat, who was overflowing the cane seat both physically and in the matter of dress. The seat wove white fingers into the mass of him, cupped hands attempting to stem a waterfall.

"This is Katerina Afanasyevna Tarsky, who acts as Jonah's prime control," Professor Kapelka introduced. "Katya, this is Comrade Orlov, from the supervisory committee. He's come about the regrettable disappearance of the Nilin child."

Orlov's vinegary eyes regarded her speculatively. Not so much pretty, as "interesting," he decided. Effervescently soulful, for a certainty. Melancholy, beneath her surface euphoria. Her full lips had a chapped, fissured texture to them; yet she was wear-

ing a coquettish trace of waxy lipstick, which she was
constantly licking at with nervous fluttering forays of
her tongue. He'd have classed her figure as slim, rather than outright skinny, but for those large dark eyes
of hers: they gave her such a waiflike appearance. The
sort of girl, in short, whom he rather liked to smother
in his coat, and body. In need of a mature man. Orlov
winked at her.

"That was careless of you," he remarked to Kapelka,
"but maybe not so unfortunate, as it turns out.
There's such panic in American life at the best of
times. You know about Hammond, of course?"

"The radio astronomer?" Kapelka inclined his head
cautiously. In fact, he knew all about the Hammond
business from blanket coverage over the American
Far East Network transmitters in northern Japan. Still,
it could be impolitic to know from such a source. He
ransacked his memory for the exact official version.
How much had *Pravda* reported? The atheistical universe was perfectly acceptable; but a nonmaterialist
cosmos which presupposed a God, even if an absent
one! That *had* to be dismissed as a mystification.
Reported dismissively.

Still, the very fact of reporting it so promptly suggested it was having impact. Needed combating.

The American radio had announced, in a breathless
dramatic way, a crazy pilgrimage to Hammond's observatory in Mexico, that ended in bloodshed and
violence. (*Pravda* concurred.)

Then, there was trouble in some Islamic countries:
demands for a jihad against the atheistical greedy
white races who only wanted to destroy faith in order
to undermine the revolutionary fervor of the Third
World. (*Pravda* deleted the middle term in this.)

Then there'd been many people crushed and tram-
pled in St. Peter's Square in Rome when the pope
had appeared on the balcony to read an encyclical
. . . (*Pravda* reported this with sarcastic relish; perhaps, in so doing, vindicating obliquely the American
claim that there were disturbances in Eastern Europe,
too, among the Catholic Poles.)

The world took Hammond seriously. He'd been right before, when he discovered the hidden galaxy colliding with the Milky Way. There'd been a flurry of popular hysteria then, for a few days, till Paul Hammond explained how "catastrophe" was a technical, mathematical term; how his newfound galaxy was seventy thousand or so light-years removed from us and much smaller than our own galaxy—and that while it might eventually distort the shape of the Milky Way, pulling free a bridge of glowing gas between the two, that event lay so far in the future that the human race would undoubtedly be extinct by then . . . and in any case stars were so far apart that one galaxy's fringes could almost pass through another's fringes with impunity. Well, Hammond had gained celebrity status, then. A deliberately engineered performance, perhaps! Nevertheless the man was swept to prominence as a pundit and remained one in the popular mind.

To be sure, the American radio reported even a baseball game as though it was a war! (And reported their wars as though they were games . . .) Yet this new discovery, and the reactions to it, certainly sounded disturbing, even filtered through *Pravda*.

"Yes, I know about it," said Kapelka.

Orlov thumped a short, square index finger on the desk. Missing its top joint, his finger ended in a stiff rubbery knob.

"Oh, the appeals to the Academy of Science from Washington! From the White House, no less. Even though Hammond supported that man's election. But our embassy tells us there is a clique against their president now who can use panic and disorder to strengthen their own position. It is those who have been helping Hammond, latterly. Wheels within wheels, eh, professor?"

"But I don't know anything about these intrigues," said Kapelka miserably, feeling increasingly—if instinctively—convinced that the Nilin boy's disappearance had been no random accident, but was part of some intrigue, too. And he had boasted to Katya about how much freedom they enjoyed in their work! When the truth was that the puppet strings were simply being kept hidden. Now they were about to be illuminated. Why else was Orlov mentioning Hammond, but to point a parallel?

"Our own Caspian and Mongolian radiotelescopes are to link up, to check Hammond's observations." Orlov rubbed his hands. "This is going to be one case where Soviet science is seen publicly to bail the Americans out."

"What if Hammond's right, though?" Kapelka asked dubiously. "Are you assuming he's wrong? Or are you planning to . . ." He hesitated.

"Falsify?" laughed Orlov. "But of course not. Suppose he is right, professor—that's ideal! The facts may be as he says—but interpretations can certainly vary. Can't you see what a coup it will be, if America is forced to adopt the same ideological position as the Soviet Union? A positive, dialectical-materialist view of the data, instead of their present mystical-pessimistic one! In point of fact, Hammond's vision of the universe can be treated perfectly adequately in Marxist terms, as a demonstration of that prime concept in dialectics, the 'negation of the negation' . . . Thus the universe, and man's role in it, are recuperated by us! And Soviet ideology is shown as what it has been all along—optimistic and humanistic—as opposed to the empty soullessness of capitalism."

"And Hammond's powerful friends will curse themselves for fools and Benedict Arnolds . . ."

"I shouldn't be surprised, professor! Oh, it's harvest time for concessions, whichever way," guffawed Orlov. "My point is, this Hammond business couldn't have come along at a better time—disturbing their sense of judgment, with Nilin on the loose. Nilin has scared them about their whole undersea security. Now Hammond forces them to beg favors. Incidentally, our sources in Japan say they're *very* worried about Nilin. It's a big fish they believe they've caught on their hook, this Jonah of yours! We shall have the boy back in no time at all, never fear. What's more, we shall force the Americans to collaborate technologically undersea, now, as a quid-pro-quo for Hammond."

"But—" How sickeningly irrelevant! Kapelka felt heartsick. Katya's news thrilled him as much as it did herself, poor girl. The Thought Complex meant something totally unsuspected on this planet. Something wonderful. But alas . . . He was older than she was.

"Maybe our Jonah is good for more than scaring people," he told Orlov icily.

"It has potential of course, I'm not denying that."

"But Jonah *swims,* Jonah *is!*"

"To be sure. But listen to me—there are political priorities right now. The Japanese are growing extremely tense and xenophobic about the oceans. It was inevitable. The likelihood of Japanese technology and Chinese manpower combining is higher now than at any time. A Co-Prosperity Sphere of the seabed . . ."

"Our own special bogey, this one, surely comrade," shrugged Kapelka. "Japan plus China. The Americans have never really believed it."

"They are beginning to see it now! The strains on the false friendship between Japan and America are telling. I admit we help this along a little. Item, the sperm-whale ban. That was a good touch. Now Nilin and the fisheries conference. But we're only really nudging inevitable historical processes. It's in this light that we've got to force American cooperation. A somewhat adjusted ideology on their part will help wonderfully, besides making us appear to the world as the dominant partner. . . . Well, we shall see, what our telescopes see."

Kapelka quit listening to the rumblings of this big black waterfall with the vinegary eyes. So Georgi Nilin had indeed been used as a pawn. And the whole whale project was regarded as similarly expendable. And had been all along? Yet Orlov hadn't actually said so outright. Kapelka still couldn't tell for the life of him whether Nilin's departure had been deliberately engineered, or only brilliantly exploited afterward.

Two games could presumably be played side by side, and both for the winning.

He smiled at Katya and reached for the bundle of perforated sheets, which she had been opening and collapsing like a silent accordion all this time, bewildered by this high-level briefing she was so privileged to listen in on. Orlov perhaps wished to impress her. Or compromise her . . .

"I must look at these a moment, Comrade Orlov—"

"How strange, Katya," mused Kapelka aloud, as he scanned the pages. "He does seem to know more of himself . . . The effect of the Thought Complex? I wonder whether its computational power is large enough to retrieve more than we were able to put into him? That would be incredible. Yet it looks that way. To think of this machine for thought, in the seas, all this time!"

"What's this, professor?" demanded Orlov, alerted. "A computer in the ocean? Whose computer? Who is it acting for?"

Kapelka smiled dryly.

"Perhaps I should have told you before. This is our greatest discovery—more important than anything we achieved with Nilin. Far more important even than the whole technique of modeling and imprinting consciousness, though we should hardly have made the discovery otherwise. . . . But I thought you came here mainly about Nilin and to wind the project down. Well?" he accused.

"You leap to conclusions, professor," Orlov said amiably. "Wide political questions are involved. I thought I made that plain. What is more vital than mastering the resources of the ocean? By whatever means! So, what is this 'Thought Complex'? Your trump card, perhaps? You must tell me this, exactly. Very rapid decisions may have to be made."

Kapelka brightened, then, seeing how the project could—and must—be salvaged.

"Ah, yes, indeed. Cachalots have this strange custom

of nosing together in a star formation on the surface of the sea. Sailors have noticed it periodically—but no one knew why they did it. Now we know. Those whales are forming themselves into a biological computer of enormous power!"

And he explained what they knew so far. And what they guessed. Confusing the two a little in the process, perhaps, deliberately . . .

"So you see, the complexes can compose sound patterns to store these mental insights!" Kapelka ended, on a ringing note. "Think of them as resembling Indian mantra meditation diagrams—that's the nearest human equivalent that comes to mind. Only, these mantra are written out purely in sound. The complexes have been evolving ever more complex mantra diagrams over tens of thousands of years—far longer than man has been seriously investigating the world. Not only that, but the whales' melons have been evolving physically in the process, to cope with these insight diagrams. And since the melon effectively operates as an adjunct to the brain, in other words, they're undergoing a very rapid, consciously directed mental evolution!"

"Your enthusiasm's laudable, professor," drawled Orlov. "And this would be magnificently useful. But does your tame whale actually report all these things? Or is there an element of educated guesswork? Which could even stretch to, say, wishful thinking? I thought your radio messages were all in a strict mathematical code."

"Yes indeed. Here—"

Kapelka spread the printout on his desk. A string of numbers was followed by the arithmetical breakdown of primes and products stretching out for a paragraph, then by several paragraphs of symbols.

Katya stared out of the window at the house where Pavel was.

Symbols to some. Realities to others . . .

And yet . . . Was Professor Kapelka simply being kind? No! He had meant what he said about what the

Thought Complex might achieve with Jonah. Therefore Pavel was saved.

If only that husk weren't still alive, to haunt her!

Yet should she wish his body dead?

"The Jonah consciousness is a mathematical model, you see," Kapelka was telling the sprawling, boorish Orlov who kept on eyeing Katya. "It's produced by detailed scanning of the neural circuitry of the live brain of a volunteer. Now, human brain and cachalot brain are fortunately topologically similar, so we are able to imprint our 'circuit diagram' on the symbolization centers of the immature baby whale. Both brains are what we call bilaterally asymmetrical. Toothed whales are the only animals apart from man to show this feature, and this all comes about because of language specialization in man and "sound symbolism' specialization in the whale."

"Whales use languages, too? I thought—"

"Ah, not languages as we understand them. Theirs is much more mimetic in character than human words and sentences. A certain wavelength X indicates 'Appearance Y.' Their click-music imitates the shape of the world in sound, whereas we attach labels to things. We're obsessed with objects. The whale is interested in flow and vector and relation. That's a radically different program from the speech program built into us humans. Yet it's still symbolic thought, articulated in organized sound! There's the point of connection. We're distant biological cousins, the whale and us."

"At so many removes, professor!"

"Yet—*still cousins*. So we can attack the problem of 'language' initially on the purely symbolic level."

Kayta stared at the smoking building with its deserted veranda, while Kapelka talked about thought, logic and mathematics. . . .

The empty veranda . . . The empty mind of the man inside the building . . . *horrifying!* Yet it drew her like a magnet!

". . . so the solid geometry of the sea shows itself to the whale's mind in a symbolic form which we may treat algebraically, as abstract neural equations in the brain. A shifting mesh of equations. The great Austrian logician Kurt Gödel devised a way of expressing complex algebraic formulae in simple numbers." Kapelka gestured at the printout. "Those are strings of Gödel numbers at the beginning. They can code algebraic statements about the 'geometrical' map Jonah is swimming through, observing, recording in his memory. They can also code the algebra for more abstract thought structures. It's on this level that we communicate with him. In plain Russian? Ah, no. Perhaps latent memories of Russian speech linger in the interstices of the personality model. I shouldn't wonder. Words, memories, any form of thought is simply a product of multidimensional matrices of cues and connections—a product of neural pathways, interacting. But human speech represents an alien transformation of symbolic thought, from the viewpoint of the whale. So we have to work with symbol structures, not the words that mediate these symbols for us."

How much of his true self carried over into the model? fretted Katya. If a man is only the sum of his neural pathways, and these are wrecked, in mapping them, then printed out elsewhere . . . how much of him is left? How much memory of her?

"So difficult!" Kapelka was saying, "To make a whale 'not a whale,' yet not a human being, either. For a human can not be a whale. To make sure that he functions efficiently, as what he is; yet to guarantee a sense of duty to humanity! Of course, the whale body has to be conditioned behaviorally. That happens before the mind is superimposed, to avoid trauma. The host has to be taught to surface on certain cues . . . Yet conditioned reflexes alone would never serve us. To truly master the seas, there must be a genuine fusion of Humanity and Marine Intelligence, on the deep symbolic level. The whale will act for us, then, because he will be one with us!"

"How far is your Jonah still 'human'?" taunted Orlov. "And how far can we trust 'him' then?"

Kayta spun around from the window.

"Oh, a lot. Such a lot. So human," she cried, and burst into tears. Orlov regarded her with amusement.

"Will you kindly leave us, Katerina Afanasyevna?" Kapelka asked her gently. "Take the printout away and produce a plain language version? I want our guest to read it, for Jonah's sake. So work well, Katya."

Twenty-one

As soon as she'd shut the door behind her, Kapelka apologized.

"I must explain about the human volunteer. I didn't like to in her presence. You see, our scanning process disrupts the neural pathways irrevocably. It's like running a tape through the record head of a tape deck and demagnetizing it. Only, not just one tape! Several hundred million of them. What it amounts to is personality erasure. That's why the volunteer has to be someone close to death, so that this is his only chance of any sort of survival. It takes courage, even so!"

Orlov stroked his amputated finger across his palm speculatively.

"And the Jonah volunteer happened to be the girl's ... husband? No, let's see, her father?"

"Neither," sighed Kapelka. "Actually, he was her lover. But only after he came here! That's the sorry part. You see, he wasn't smashed up like Cosmonaut Nilin. He had a cancer."

"Ah—"

"His name was Pavel Chirikov. A man blind from birth. Can you guess why we chose a blind man?"

"A keener appreciation of sounds," Orlov responded in a bored tone. "A musician, wasn't he?"

"So you already know all about him, do you!"

"Well, something, obviously," laughed Orlov. "But not about what went on here between him and the Tarsky girl. That part interests me . . . It's understandable, the girl's reaction. This Chirikov is physically dead—yet something of his mind lingers on in the Jonah whale. . . . But I wonder, doesn't this severely prejudice her scientific objectivity? This Thought Complex matter—so wonderful if it were true. Maybe it has to be true, for her? I wonder whether she is the best prime control? I shall have to have a word with her. To assess her." He smiled.

"Obviously you don't know everything, comrade!" snapped Kapelka, in a fury. "The scanning took place eighteen months ago. The man is still alive. Eating, sleeping, shitting, thumb-sucking like a baby! His body's still with us—it won't die! The shock of the scanning operation on his whole nervous system apparently retarded the cancer. . . ." Kapelka stared out of the window, too, at that nearby house.

"But cancer isn't a nervous disorder, professor," rebuked Orlov. "Even I know that. It's organic."

"The psychic shock must have pepped up his immune system, nevertheless. Look at it this way, comrade. Nowadays we regard a disease like muscular dystrophy as representing a massive rejection of its own nervous system, by the body. The immune system going haywire. In Chirikov's case, from the immune system's point of view, the scanning must have seemed like a huge alienation of all the higher nervous functions—which triggered a countermeasure . . . which only had the physical cancer as a target. That's the only feasible explanation. Anyhow, as a result, the body called Pavel Chirikov is still dragging out a sort of vegetable existence. Which is very painful for Katya Tarsky. She sees the body, to all appearances alive. Yet the mind is far away, imprinted in an alien beast. But is it his mind? Or only a partial model of his mind? Which is the real Pavel? Or are both unreal? What a dilemma. His body needs pain killers now. It's beginning to show intense distress without them. So it'll still die. But so long as it lives . . . well, he was a hero, wasn't he, volunteering for the project?"

Orlov shrugged and directed the subject back to whales.

And Kapelka told him something else he had been saving—told him somewhat hopelessly, yet with defiance: their Jonah had signaled to them that the sperm whales knew how to use the baleen whales as long-range trans-ocean transmitters. . . .

The black waterfall boomed: "You mean to say you have a system for sending messages all the way across the Pacific underwater? In a virtually unbreakable nonlanguage code? Why haven't you reported this earlier, professor?"

"First you accuse me of reading too much into the Thought Complex reports. Now you want to know why we haven't rushed out a report."

"It is *relevant*," muttered Orlov, thumping his chin with his finger stub. "If only the Americans weren't alerted, damn it! And yet, and yet—it could serve our purpose well. Supposing—" But he didn't continue the sentence. For the first time since his arrival, he seemed somewhat overtaken by events, and Kapelka felt the spark of hope rekindle in himself.

"Unfortunately, Comrade Orlov, you can't disconnect the long-range transmitter aspect from the Thought Complex. Since it seems to be mainly these mantra—these mental insights, the Whale Philosophy —that the baleen whales broadcast for the cachalots . . ."

"Is that true? And this Thought Complex is really a kind of super-computer, linked in to an oceanwide communications network?" Tap, tap, on his chin.

"The human brain is far more complex than any computer. The whale brain is equally complex. What mightn't a union of seven such brains be! Thought to the seventh power? Isn't it wonderful, comrade?"

"Yes . . . Tell me, would this Thought Complex be able to compute other kinds of problems? If your Jonah joins it, and we feed him the data?"

Kapelka nodded, afraid not to agree.

"But what problems? The original plan was to use the Jonah whale and his successors for intelligence work. Undersea surveillance."

"Well, this would be intelligence work in the literal sense," laughed Orlov. "If this brain-complex is so superior to a computer—and we have the best American computer available here . . . then we have the best means of processing all this Hammond astrophysics data. I said the implacable forces of history are on our side, didn't I, professor! But will your whale really accept input that has nothing to do with the sea or ships or submarines? That's what I'm asking."

"If the information can be coded mathematically, then I don't see why not. Mathematics is a universal language of structures, rather than contents. So if this data can be presented as an abstract structure . . ."

"It'll be a new 'mantra' for them," Orlov said simply.

Perhaps, thought Kapelka; but he didn't wish to argue.

"One thing that's germane to that, professor. How exactly does your Jonah handle his Gödel Code? Numbers like two hundred and forty-three million. I saw that on the computer sheet. It would take me half an hour to work it out!"

"It's just the product of certain prime numbers, raised to a certain power. That one's 2^6 times 3^5 times 5^6 . . . I happen to know that particular one, but an idiot savant could compute it in half a second without conscious effort on his part. There are such people, you know! Possibly you've heard of my case study of the 'Uzbek Boy'? The brain is a magnificent computer, but we don't know how to run it, really. It runs us most of the time. So we've programmed an 'idiot savant' capacity into our Jonah model. It's perfectly compatible with his own thought processes. After all, they're simply a mathematical model, too. It's as natural a reaction for him to turn data into Gödel numbers as for us opening our mouths for food. You're not aware of the act of eating, are you? Only of the food itself . . ." Kapelka's eyes pecked away at Orlov's sprawling girth. "In point of fact, we diverted some of the Purkinje learning cells in the cerebellum for this. Periodically the implanted radio sets up a certain level of excitation. To him, it'll feel like muscle cramps in the very small area of his neck that these particular cells would otherwise be operating."

"Ingenious—a subconscious overseer . . ."

Kapelka shook his head.

"Not a subconscious one, no. Jonah's subconscious . . . well, as to that, there may be a whale 'subconscious' in the sense of the repressed, overprinted personality of the animal we captured and conditioned. Perhaps a human subconscious, too—trace elements of the former man that aren't a strong enough component of the model to register consciously." He steepled his hands, and fell silent, lost in thought.

Orlov stood up abruptly, setting the cane chair squealing against the wooden tiles. Though it was warm enough in the office, he dragged his black coat about him densely.

"I shouldn't worry, professor." He rubbed his hands jubilantly. "A very heartening discussion. We have those poor Americans over a barrel," he chuckled.

Katya Tarsky ran breathlessly through the bamboo thicket. The thin stems arched overhead, weaving a dense tunnel. Halting just before the exit into the open, in a place where she could watch the nearby house without exposing herself to view, she sank to the ground on a dry moss tussock, and tried to concentrate all her attention on the printout, scribbling on a pad she took from her overalls.

A certain number, running to several millions, had been broken down by the 370–185 into the product of its primes . . .

$2^2 \times 3^8 \times 5^4$ . . .

Which was followed, further down the page, by certain corresponding logic symbols . . .

ℲQR . . .

Which in turn translated into Russian as: "There is/a composite/greater than/the sum of/individual units . . ."

She wrote on the pad:

"The Thought Complex—definition. Refers to a situation where a number (7) of whale brains link up in parallel, generating a state of mental insight far beyond their normal powers. . . ."

But alas, where was the music of the sea? Where was the magic of the whale's existence that Pavel had sought so fearfully, and so deliriously? It wasn't here in cold words, cold symbols!

The veranda door opened; an attendant wheeled out a bathchair into the sunshine.

She didn't want to see its occupant too closely.

Shaven-headed. Shrunken. Drooling like a baby— with as rudimentary control over his bowels as any baby.

His ears would register sounds without being able to know what they meant. Without even being able to understand that there was something to be understood; so frozen in a state of unknowing was he! So lowly in the scale of life now, that cancer halted in bewilderment at what it was bothering to attack!

She sat and wept instead of scribbling. Was he really contained in these formalities from thousands of miles away? Or was he nowhere, except in her memory?

Feet vibrated the moss behind her. A bulky mass trying to tread softly . . . Then Orlov thumped down beside her, and the earth rocked on impact.

"You are sad, skinny little one—"

"Why did you follow me, Comrade Orlov?"

"Why, to know about Jonah," he protested, with wounded innocence, stretching out the hand with the amputated finger, to pat her cheek.

His coat . . . So huge, so blanketing—on such a warm day!

To burrow . . . To forget . . .

Twenty-two

Kimble gave a token knock on Hammond's door before stepping inside, wondering which of the two would lose his temper first.

Spying all the newspapers and magazines spread lavishly across Paul's desk, Richard decided most likely it would be himself. So that was what the helicopter had flown in with. Paul's press clippings.

The crew-cut individual with the bright blue tie welded round his neck must be the procurer of these scraps of megalomania fodder.

There lay *Time* with Paul's face as its cover painting. And enough front pages with his features on them to paper the office walls. *Saint-Louis Post Dispatch, L'Osservatore Romano, Die Zeit, Chicago Daily News* . . . five dozen papers at least.

Other lead stories—another radioactive iceberg loose off Cape Horn—the Dow Jones index dipping below the 400 mark—the anthrax epidemic in the Philippines—items of daily horror that could be summed up simply as the human race running headlong into a brick wall as thick as the rest of history, did not seem so much to have been shoved aside by Paul, as incarnated in his image.

"So you've made *Time* again!" Richard ignored Paul's presumed courier. "It's sort of uglier than last time. Pity. That cost a few lives at the barricade. And elsewhere! How many thousand lives will the second Nobel Prize add up too, I wonder? Ah, you've got *L'Osservatore Romano*? What's the Vatican's view of scientific nihilism?"

Hammond smiled faintly at his own reflection multiplied before him.

"Certainly you may borrow Kimble, Mr. Mercer," he remarked in the vague direction of the man with the strangling necktie. "A word of advice, though. Don't subject him to too much stress. As you can see, it's very hard to maintain composure in the face of really big discoveries. Even Galileo rubbed his eyes when he first saw the rings of Saturn. Though he opened them wide again, to his credit. Alas that public opinion wasn't so receptive in his day—

"Richard," he beamed, focusing at last on a human face other than his own, "it appears that your *jeu d'esprit* in the *Worm Runners' Digest* has borne fruit. You're about to become a man of the moment, too, in your own way!"

"We read your piece in the *Biological Psychology* magazine, sir," Mercer interposed hastily. "You may hold the key to an awkward situation. I don't want to say too much about it right now." He contrived a grimace at Paul, without Paul's noticing, that heartily endeared him to Richard.

And he called the *Journal* by its serious title! Even if he did get the words jumbled up . . . Which meant —that someone had taken his article seriously? But in whatever context

Seeing Richard on the point of asking questions, Gerry Mercer shook his head firmly, nodding toward the door. He seemed anxious to be on his way.

"Of course, we had our doubts about you," Gerry admitted during the flight to the city. "Being one of

Hammond's men. Look what you're responsible for—"

His gesture embraced the mad shantytown now trailing a couple of miles from the soldiers. Smoke drifted up from burned-out cars up front . . .

"Medieval! An idiots' crusade! I hear you accused him of murder, in the end?"

"He shot a man, to start a riot. I saw it. He didn't actually hold the gun—that wouldn't be Paul's style. A soldier wanted to loose off a warning shot. Paul's bitch of a wife was cockteasing some Hell's Angel across the barbed wire, and Paul deliberately grabbed the soldier's arm at the vital moment so the shot wouldn't miss. I call that murder."

"We've already asked the Soviet Academy of Sciences to check out some of his findings—for a price. They tally, damn it. The Russians can't fault him. . . ."

"It's almost as though we have no choice—can't observe anything else," mused Richard, Morelli's remarks still printed freshly on his mind. "What we observe from now on has been determined. We've chosen out of a whole set of possible branches of reality, so this is the branch that exists for us from now on—a branch where consensus reality equals unreality and despair. If he'd waited till Seattle, there might have been alternatives. But he released just enough to tease the world's imagination—the most malign hellbent streak in it. Somehow it seems to have changed events objectively. We're all participators in this madness now. Do you understand me, Gerry? That a collective act of choice can change the objective world, so that even the Russians get the same signals from their radio dishes?"

"Search me." Gerry shook his head. "It could be in the Soviet interest to promote loss of confidence in the West. They may be lying. On the other hand, why offer to let us run Hammond's findings through this secret whale computer of theirs? Maybe it's all a game with them. Orville Parr thinks so. My boss. Still, they're having trouble in Eastern Europe, on account of Hammond. Catholic and Jewish 'dissidents' burning party headquarters—as a sort of way of exorcizing atheism, I suppose. They were rioting about food prices last year. We're both tarred with the same brush now, we and the Soviets, I guess. We need each other."

Richard rounded on Mercer, bewildered.

"What whale computer?"

So then Gerry Mercer told him. About Georgi Nilin. About Sakhalin. About the biological computer in the ocean, code-named the Thought Complex, that the Russians apparently had access to.

"But that's fantastic. It's as important as Hammond's Footsteps. No! Much more so. It's big enough —it could save the world from this madness."

"Equally, it could all be a fake."

"If another intelligent species observes the Footsteps Theorem—if we can pass it over to them—they could make a different choice! They could shift the branch we're out on, before it snaps right off!"

It was Mercer's turn to confess bewilderment.

So Richard explained about Schrödinger's Cat, locked up with that bottle of prussic acid with the hammer poised over it. The cat's cage seemed a true image of the world to him at this moment. And the hammer was already in process of falling—triggered by the vibrations of Paul's Footsteps.

Might those footsteps be unwalked—by wise beasts of the ocean who had shed their limbs a hundred million years ago? Who therefore had no need of footprints, even maybe of gods, absent or present?

Only later on in the flight, when they'd switched from the helicopter to an executive jet and were speeding toward Hawaii en route to Hokkaido, did he think to ask how "the agency" had got the data to pass over to the Russians—data which Hammond had deliberately refrained from publishing properly yet.

Gerry Mercer grinned.

"Good luck, mainly. I've only come in on the tail end of this part, but it seems the third man at your observatory—what's his name, Berg?—has been send-

ing it all off fast to a physicist friend in California,
Avram something-or-other. Some fellow immigrant.
But *sub rosa*—confidentially. Berg was scared of
something or other unpleasant happening months ago.
Maybe his name not getting connected with the
work?"

"That I doubt!"

"Well, he couldn't have foreseen all this present
fuss. I guess a dose of Nazi persecution makes a man
a bit paranoid. Anyhow, this Avram person's in a sensitive area—laser fusion research—and he still has an
old Momma back in Eastern Europe, you know the
sort of thing. It's routine—our people keep a casual
eye on him. We logged a whole lot of mail coming
from Mezapico. Then what do you know, this Avram
came to us a week ago with all the data?"

"Max must have told him to," brooded Richard, realizing how little occasion Max had ever really had to
trust him. How lonely Max must have felt all these
months, while Richard played around with Ruth, and
was Paul's man. The information curdled inside him
progressively, like stale milk, the more he considered
it.

"Oh, incidentally, too, we must tell Hammond we
have the data and what we're going to do with it."

"He doesn't know "

"Uh-uh. From all I hear about him, he'll be only too
happy to make out it was his own idea in the first
place, if we give him that facesaver."

"More lousy publicity."

"Right. But that's why I hurried you out—him not
knowing yet. You see, we have to make out *you* gave
us the data, Dr. Kimble."

"Me!"

"Sure, to cover up for your colleague Berg. We'd
like to keep him where he is."

"But Max is a free agent. *You* don't keep him. It's
not *your* say-so whether he stays at Mezapico or not."

"Quite. It's Hammond's. And Hammond would fire
him if he found out who was responsible. And this
Berg's a useful ear on friend Hammond, whether he

knows it or not. You don't mind, do you? Obviously you won't be going back to work with Hammond again. You weren't exactly polite during the brief time I was there. But we'll see that you're not blackballed. A professorship someplace—we can fix it. Not that you won't deserve it, if you help crack this business. Whale computers and variable universes—we need assistance, friend!"

Twenty-three

At the last moment before they took off from Wakkanai for the hundred mile hop across La Pérouse Strait, Georgi Nilin broke free from Mikhail and ran to Orville Parr—who was traveling no farther. Burrowing in his coat, the boy clung to him, pleading and cursing in a gabble of Russian and English. He seemed an enraged pigmy more than a little boy, or an intelligent piglet about to be slaughtered. The thin reedy voice rose to the pitch of a whistle, squealing for asylum.

Parr ruffled the child's fair spiky hair, hugging him. Uncontrollable trembling transmitted itself through his own insulating layers of fat, and it wasn't the dawn chill that made the boy shake.

How absurd, he thought—how pathetically tender, too!—if this really is a full-grown man I'm cuddling here, giving the last love he'll surely get. How submissive and downtrodden Mikhail seemed by comparison, accepting the handing back resignedly—the trudge to a labor camp. Maybe only as far as a pockmarked prison yard and a shallow lime-strewn grave

163

hacked out of the rock-hard soil as his last human activity before obliteration . . . Damn it, he took it too submissively! He ought to be raging, like the boy. Squealing. Pleading. Not standing slumped like the eternal peasant waiting for a flogging. Shit, he had had the wit and initiative to escape in the first place!

"This thing stinks," Parr confided to the boy. "We're handing you back, now that we *know* you're genuine, and that Mikhail, who brought you all this way for safety and a new life, won't even raise a finger. He could at least try a getaway across the airstrip with you tucked under his arm. But if you're so real, and he's not genuine, then what the hell mess is this we've got ourselves into?"

The boy babbled helplessly against him.

"Gerry, come here a minute," he called, his breath hanging out in a speech bubble in the chill air, words recorded implacably by the landscape. . . .

"Gerry, if I told you this whole operation ought to be halted—that the boy's genuine enough, but the whole thing is a rotten mistake, would you think the old man was losing his grip?"

"At this point we're committed! It's too late."

Gently, Gerry detached the struggling boy from Parr's body, little hands clutching fiercely at his overcoat, having to be unplucked finger by finger.

"Let's hope Tom Winterburn keeps his eyes open," offered Parr hopefully, feeling little personal hope. "Though he's already disposed in favor of this mind-transplant caper. Herb Flynn's a skeptic. Kimble—you say he's pretty embittered."

"But not about whales!" Gerry shouted over the boy's squeals, lifting him bodily off the ground, feet kicking. "That's the only thing that seems to matter to him at the moment. . . . Hey, this part *is* kind of vile, Orville, surrendering the kid like this. Tell you what, let's get a few drinks under our belt, as soon as the plane's left. You on?"

"Sure," agreed Parr dourly. "And—thanks, Gerry," he added. "For taking the kid. I couldn't have. I guess Enozawa's crab fleets can set sail now."

They were met at the administrative capital, Yuzhno-Sakhalinsk, by a voluminous Russian named Orlov, and a thin dark-haired girl called Tarsky who seemed to be doing her best to treat Orlov as a contagious disease.

Richard Kimble gazed at her in surprise, and with a joy of recognition. She was Ruth—a pained, hurt Ruth, yet without Ruth's vacuumlike hollowness and deceptiveness. She was the soul Ruth should have had inside her. The dab of Russian lipstick she was wearing looked so cheap, and incompetently administered: aching adolescence prolonged far beyond its normal cut-off point. Any lipstick was probably hard to get hold of here. Richard found himself wishing he could have known, to bring some present for her. Lipstick, yes. Hers looked like grease to keep the cold off her chapped lips. Her hair was a beautiful crinkly chaos. Her eyes, so tired and sore, were nevertheless shining with a hurt and exhaustion that she'd somehow converted into a source of joy.

She was like Ruth, yet wasn't Ruth at all. Was, rather, the authentic Ruth (whom Ruth had only poorly impersonated) which is to say, the idea, the image, the anima in Richard's mind.

"Professor Kapelka asked me to greet you," the girl said in accented, glutinous English. English with thick sauce added.

"So that's our runaway?" growled Orlov.

Georgi had frozen as soon as the flight began and had to be carried off the plane in Tom Winterburn's arms.

"He's our responsibility," the girl said sharply in Russian, but overheard by Winterburn. "The institute's. You can't punish a six-year-old for running away."

"Quite right, little one," Orlov grinned. "Since he's only a mathematical model—like Jonah, eh? How can one punish a mathematical model?"

The girl flushed and bit her lip.

"But why speak of punishments? How boorish to punish anybody, when Nilin's escapade has brought us together with our American friends on such a splendid scientific undertaking! A rendezvous as momentous as any Salyut-Spacelab link up, eh? More so!"

Orlov shifted from Russian to English halfway through this rebuke, nodding amiably at the new arrivals.

"Mikhail, however," he told the girl, reverting to Russian "must at least be interviewed—surely you realize that. Perhaps found another, less sensitive task ... Or maybe back to Ozerskiy with him? Who knows? It might be psychologically damaging to Nilin—Mikhail being his only friend—to be deprived . . ." He wagged a stubby finger at Katya Tarsky. "Yes, why not back to Ozerskiy But first of all, a talking-to!"

A pair of waiting security men sidled up to Mikhail and said something in his ear, before marching off with him. Mikhail appeared almost bored by the proceedings. Winterburn watched his expression curiously, trying to fathom the difference between resignation and complicity.

"Let me carry the child." Orlov removed the burden from the naval attaché and hefted the boy onto his shoulder. This way, gentlemen. We have some cars waiting. Lead on, little one. You will ride with the boy. The feminine sisterly touch, I think."

"Take Nilin in the first car yourself," she snapped back. "I trust you to deliver him. I must talk about whales to the Americans."

The argument was conducted loudly in English, as though the girl wanted to make as strong a point as possible, and didn't care about the consequences.

Winterburn confided, "I think Parr was right, in a sense. The boy *was* bait. Probably they wanted to scare us about the deep-sub—because the genuine marine payoff from their Jonah Kit seemed too slow in coming. They'd decided to shut the project down as a drain on resources. Use the computer for something else, and Nilin as a *cause célèbre*: which, let's be frank, he's been damned effective as. Then up comes this Thought Complex, and they're really onto something

. . . but they've blown their cover by now. Then this Hammond business erupts in the midst of it all and they see a way to recoup their original stakes, as well as rake in the winnings. And we're genuinely grateful. We come cap in hand."

"We'd better make damn sure this Thought Complex isn't just some clever computer sham." Herb Flynn raked his welt-strewn face violently. "I shall insist they make their whale appear—solidly in the living blubber!"

"If that big fellow is one of the ones who set the boy up as bait, then that girl's a pretty courageous lady, it seems to me," Richard said, as Katya Tarsky impatiently gestured them to come along.

"You'll have to find that one out for yourself, won't you?" smiled Winterburn, patting the astronomer on the shoulder. "I can see you want to. You're transparent."

Richard shivered as they stepped out of the Moskvitch saloon at Ozerskiy. An hour's drive had brought them through snow-pocked forests to the reeking, smoky port of Korsakov and on along the sparser shore. Scudding rain showers lashed the windows twice as they drove. The road was slippery with mud, and initially they shared it with timber trucks wearing tires as high as the cars themselves.

"You're cold?" asked Katya, surprised, for the mild spell still hadn't broken.

"Just a bit, Miss Tarsky. Or is it Dr. Tarsky? Or don't you use titles much? I mean, personally I'd prefer it if you called me Richard—"

"You may call me Katya. Best to ignore my *familiya* —though colleagues generally use it. But I have really forgotten about my father, so it's silly adding his name to mine. Besides it's an ugly name—Afanasyevna, don't you think?"

Richard grinned.

"It's . . . fat and flabby. Like a washerwoman with huge red arms. You're not at all like that!"

She giggled delightedly.

"I've got a silly middle name, too," he confessed. "My folks came from Europe. They were so glad to join in the American way of life that they gave me Edison for a middle name."

"The inventor Thomas Alva Edison? There are worse names! At least it made a scientist out of you."

"It's embarrassing. You get laughed at in school—asked to invent the electric light or something."

The black coastline, with its clusters of buildings, backed onto sparse pine groves and bamboo clumps thickening into denser leaf cover on hills beyond thin, sloping meadows . . .

"Bamboo? In this temperature?"

"A hardy strain. Besides, it's warm today, Richard. But I'm forgetting, you coming from Mexico—such a way!"

She gazed meditatively out across the gray sea.

He gambled a guess at the thin girl's thoughts.

"Your Jonah's a long way off, too, isn't he, Katya? Will you tell me his real name?"

She hesitated briefly.

"Pavel Chirikov. But don't ask me any more about him. Talk about Jonah only. Jonah is a mathematical model of a consciousness, as Comrade Orlov was kind enough to point out."

"If a model is accurate enough, how do you tell it from reality?" he asked gently.

"Please!" she begged, catching hold of his hand briefly and pressing it, and him, into silence.

Nilin sat on Orlov's knee in the professor's office, lost in withdrawn stupor, the Mongol cast of his features more pronounced than ever now. They hovered on the verge of imbecility. Crew-cut scrap of a pathetic stray, he'd given up the fight for intelligence along with his other struggle to escape. Orlov, holding him, was a fat unscrupulous Dickensian beadle.

After drinking toasts to cooperation and a Soviet-American whale, out of conical glasses without bases that had to be drained before they could be set down, upside down, they sat listening while Kapelka talked about problems of mapping and imprinting, in a precise, chirrupy style of English. He had what Leonardo would have characterized as a bird physiognomy, reflected Richard. Sharp, alert, worm-pecking features—swooping on facts and winkling them out of the mud—but with a humorous glint in his eye. If Dr. Paul was a suntanned, shock-haired vulture, this man was a blackbird or thrush.

". . . So Kurt Gödel proved that a mathematical system cannot completely describe itself, yes? The same restriction necessarily applies to a complete account of consciousness considered as a mathematical system. We therefore abstract from the whole, a model which will be the most serviceable approximation. Incompleteness is an inescapable element. The model is a subsystem of a meta-system. It isn't clear how much of the omission could be retrieved—by a higher-order approach."

Meanwhile, the last vodka stains percolated from the inverted glasses down the wormholes in the professor's desk.

"Consciousness is the dialectical product of Brain and World," grumbled Orlov. "You seem to be hunting for a soul, almost. 'Something that Science cannot describe.'"

"Not at all! Please read Gödel's Proof before you judge. I'm simply talking about restrictions inherent in the logic of mathematics."

"And if a different level of consciousness inspected the model?" pressed Katya anxiously. "That would be a *meta*-mathematical inspection, wouldn't it? And consequently—" She darted a look of scorn at Orlov.

"Yes, the Thought Complex may constitute such a higher-order system," nodded Kapelka.

"Comrade Professor," chided Orlov, "we decided yesterday that this Thought Complex should be designated the *Zvezdaja Mysl* from now on, did we not?" He wagged a stubby pink finger at the visitors. "Which means 'Thought Star.' Those are names of two of the great revolutionary newspapers which played such a major role in the evolution of political consciousness in this country."

"Thought Star, then," Kapelka acquiesced. "Now, the second difficulty, my American friends, is this: we can map our model only onto a relatively blank framework. Which necessarily means an infant, whether human, or whale! The input has to be by way of immature pathways, still largely vacant."

Tom Winterburn leaned forward eagerly, sucking in his cheeks cadaverously.

"We guessed as much. But doesn't the infant brain develop irregularly? So you can record your model all at once in the computer, but imprint it only by stages?"

"Indeed. Now, doing so may accelerate brain development in some areas. Then again, this may abort some aspects of natural growth. Witness Nilin here. Picturesquely, you could say that the brain is too busy laying down new roads, under these circumstances, to build enough new houses along all of them. The boy is, on the map at least, a full-scale 'adult' town. Call it Nilingrad. Yet many of that town's houses are only stage scenery. Their doors won't open—"

"And their windows have no views," exclaimed Richard. In painful detail he recalled a certain conversation on a clifftop, not so long ago.

"Exactly!" Kapelka clapped his hands gleefully. "But we learned a lot from Nilin. And the whale brain develops faster than the human. Its 'switching-on' program is quicker than ours, though no less sophisticated. *Jonahgrad* is inevitably a queer town, hardly designed for human beings to inhabit. Yet it isn't necessarily uninhabitable, for that reason. Undoubtedly novel cognitive syntheses will take place, as our map and its territory fuse together. Remember too, we still have to communicate with our symbolic map, rather than with its territory. The actual wonderful buildings of this new City of Mind we can, alas, only guess at."

"Because we need those buildings to see their partner buildings from," said Richard, excited. "They're invisible from our own buildings. Our windows have the wrong sort of glass in them."

Taking his spectacles off, he blinked at them thoughtfully.

"It's as though reality is a set of different cities all occupying the same site . . . as though Byzantium, Constantinople and Istanbul all coexist at once. Yet the citizens of any one of them can't see the others. How wonderful to look through those other windows!"

"Jonah has looked," Katya affirmed.

"It may be terrible to see through such windows," Orlov suggested dourly. "Are you not trying to escape that fate right now, Americans? Your radiotelescope is your window. The view is bleak and frightful to you. Yet you can't stop yourselves adopting it. *Anything* is preferable to that view! Any price worth paying to substitute Jonah's window!" Whether he was gloating, or genuinely moved, was hard to tell.

When the professor had clapped his hands in glee, just then—that pocking, burping smack of a sound . . . Richard remembered: it was the noise of windows popping out of a new skyscraper, plucked out by a wind generated in part by the shape of the building itself. . . .

Chicago. Five years earlier. The thin, winged pyramid of the new Pharaoh Insurance Building had suddenly become a deathtrap one day when the wind blew in from a particular direction over Lake Michigan, and people were sucked to their deaths from twenty floors below the cantilevered Asgard and Olympus Restaurants.

Richard was in the windy city on the day the windows popped; saw them fluttering down on gusts of the building's own sculpting—like sparkling bird feathers at first, then as they dived into the streets, no longer feathers of birds, but plunging transparent knives, lethal scalpels from the sky. And people fled, the cars collided in half-mile tailgates.

Thirty or forty bodies fell from the sky in this static air disaster, yet it was the sight of the glass beaks he remembered most, pecking the streets . . . and the eerie wail.

Afterward, the new skyscraper had to be shuttered with steel all around its midriff, and no one would rent those offices again. They stayed empty.

Impulsively, he described to them all that day when the windows rained from the Chicago sky, leaving a gap-eyed monolith: rack on rack of skull eyes supporting the twin-winged restaurants.

"And the sound, afterward! Till they could weld over the empty windows, the building played like a vile harmonica—a screech that set everyone's teeth on edge. You could hear it howling for miles: the great void building whistling to itself across the city, worse than any nuclear siren."

The memory of those windows falling had been a recurrent nightmare of Richard's for a year after the event. Sometimes he was on one side of the glass. Sometimes the other. Sometimes, worst of all, he was the glass itself, bending under intolerable suction, till it pocked and flew down.

What if the human mind itself, post-Hammond, was becoming such an untenable building—while the Mezapico Dish let out its silent howl around the world?

Katya touched Richard on the arm.

"Pavel was a musician, a sound-maker," she whispered confidentially. "I shall tell you about him, later. I promise. You'll understand, I can see now."

"But what if there are windows that can't exist in certain buildings?" he asked sadly. "Are you certain you can reconcile our own 'logic' with the way the whale sees things?"

Kapelka shook himself free of this vision of a windowless city of the mind, disinterring some more fat worms of fact.

"The speech problem, yes, a good point," he chirped. "All our higher mental functions take place on the basis of human speech. Why, we even learn to *see* with the aid of our brain's language-processing equipment. But characteristically the human sentence *ma-*

nipulates objects and events—in the literal sense. Apprehension is *prehension*: the hand reaching out to grasp. Of course, whales have no hands, no artifacts, no manufactures. There need be no reaching out and grasping, to relate our whale to the world. Nor the distancing of his mind from the world, by a hand's breadth, which makes us technologists and scientists, taking things apart and putting them together."

"Alienating us from reality in the process, I wonder?" queried Richard. "So that we end up in our turn by literally alienating reality itself?"

"It may be," nodded Kapelka. "Perhaps since the whale lacks hands, his mind may conceive a far greater identity of thought, with things. There may be no 'things' as such for him, but only 'states of being.' Yet we can reconcile symbolic logic and cetacean logic. That is in fact the answer to the speech problem. Logic, of course, is a grid without specific content. A formalization of a mode of thought. But, for a start, if you are ingenious, you can say a lot with formal concepts in themselves. You can, in effect, create a type of *meta*-vocabulary out of formal signs: a topology of thought. Logic in fact is ideally designed to express the function-object relation prevailing between objects— far better than popular language—and this is what whales express: modalities, function relations. Admittedly we were forced to program a minimal 'vocabulary', a conditioned reflex association of symbols with certain objects." He glanced covertly at Orlov who was, however, lost in some private reverie of his own. "Such as submarines, you see? But not the word 'submarine.' Rather, mental markers associated with certain arbitrarily chosen numbers: a mini-calculus, if you like, within the formal framework. It isn't possible to have a totally *formal* language. It might be elegant, yet it would express nothing. But, from one axiom many axioms may grow. Likewise, our minimal vocabulary crystallizes out symbols across the interface of whale and human, as it were in a seeding operation —and refers back to this interface again, so that we can truly reach across the barrier into the whale mind, using largely formal tools."

"I take my hat off to you, sincerely, Professor Kapelka," flushed Herb Flynn. "Without reservation. You *have* found the key!"

"Thus, Dr. Kimble," beamed Kapelka, "we do believe we have sufficient glass of the right strength and refractive index in our scheme of mathematical logic to provide a two-way window between the symbols of the whale and those of man. A window that will not wrench loose in the storms of the sea!"

Richard nodded, enthralled.

Orlov, however, was starting to feel afraid. He scented a dangerous mental enzyme at work here, that could break down the whole metabolism of logical, dialectical thought. It was other than what he had thought, and recommended to the supervisory committee. It was an error feeding the blatantly negative, mystical Hammond Theorem into the Thought Star, he decided. He couldn't exactly express why. A hunch. And it was too late to put a stop to it. The Americans were here. The deals had been made.

As Orlov shifted uneasily in his seat, Georgi Nilin's stubby head nodded slackly to one side, losing all tone. He shook the boy, revolted; but the head only rocked like driftwood at the tideline. The boy wasn't dead, or even asleep; just disengaged. He had slipped across some interface, further into nowhere.

The light burden of his body crushed Orlov now. Never before in his life had he felt himself so weighed down—so useless. The American madness was robbing him of purpose. He was responsible for the Nilin "defection," yes! Mikhail had performed as instructed. Yet the world had shifted, under Orlov's feet, in the midst of the dance of deceit. He had the horrible illusion now of having been relocated abruptly to one of those other houses the bespectacled American spoke about: suddenly mode-shifted from a Leningrad to a Petersburg where all the views were different and the Revolution was reversed; where the dialectical process had spun backward, against the flow of time and history, a raw absolute antithesis.

Orlov's great black coat froze around him, under the pressure of this little boy. Then the illusion faded. The boy grew light again—almost weightless.

Twenty-four

Richard Kimble and Katya Tarsky walked through the wooded hills, a sense of delight at the existence of the Thought Star lacing their thoughts together. Richard wished it could as easily enlace their fingertips, but didn't stretch his hand the necessary inches, sensing that it wasn't what the skinny girl wanted, yet.

She said of the Star of Thought, the *Zvezdaja Mysl*:

"*Sobornost* is one Russian word for 'togetherness.' A beautiful name. So rich and trusting. Yet it has dark colors in it, too. The sharing of sorrow also."

She pointed out the different species of trees to him. The silver firs. Manchurian cedars with their blue cones. Many larch and spruce. Some birch. Some maple and cork oak. Deciduous types took over from conifers the farther inland they walked. Between the trees, with their pocket handkerchiefs of snow, a few dog roses still bore flowers, chilled and preserved: slight blooms reminding him of the pink eye of albino rabbits, so close to the white fluffiness of snow. Thick thistle patches clumped here and there—glaucous northerly versions of the Mexican cacti.

And Richard said, "I thought it would all be bare.
Yet Mexico is the barren country, with all the life
baked out of it. It's beautiful here, Katya!"

"Sakhalin's a long island: thirteen hundred kilome-
ters, Richard, and we're right in the south. The northern
half's arctic enough. Mercury freezes in the ther-
mometer. There's tundra, sea ice . . . We're on the
same latitude as Milan in Europe, would you believe?
Siberia's an icebox with an open door, just over there,
so it isn't like Italy. Not that I know Italy! Have you
been to Italy? But the sea warms us. The cachalots
swim further north than this. To Okhotsk and the Ber-
ing Sea."

They spoke of the valleys of the sea that Jonah
would be swimming through: the contour lines
marked out for him in jellyfish and squid instead of
conifers and maples.

And they spoke of man, reconstructed by the Star.
What was the texture of Jonah's consciousness now?
Apprehension, *plus* prehension: a new skyscraper with
firm new windows on reality—along with the old human ones—a four-dimensional building, almost.

And through the alien windows, with the Thought
Star's help, a different insight upon Hammond's bleak
cosmos surely could be gleaned. When the Star
grasped the new data thrust into Jonah's mind at the
crucial moment—when it surveyed the symbolic theorem of space-time culled from holes in the edge of the
universe, there would come into being a fresh view,
with fresh observers. Fresh *participants*.

Thereafter, such possibilities of an embassy of minds
on the deep symbolic level! Of a general, grammar of
existence for the Earth-and-Sea. Of *Homo physeter*, a
new mental breed swimming the oceans. Of *Physeter
sapiens* striding out of the sea bringing ocean music
to a needy, desiccated land. . . . They rhapsodized
somewhat, as they walked. Many possibilities lay open,
on that chilly autumn day, on the Russian island.

Katya halted in the lee of a spruce copse, where
snow lay a few inches thick, porous and poachy from
half-melting. Kneeling, she pressed mushy tubes in

it with her fingertips as though hunting for something.
But there was nothing underneath except the brown
mud with which her fingers emerged, stained.

"Pavel never saw the sea or the trees or my own
face," she told him. "But his ears brought him all the
world. He could pay any wind instrument, almost—
flute, clarinet . . . He played the clarinet professionally
for Irkutsk Symphony Orchestra, then jazz saxophone
in a student club in the city. He made a few public
recordings with the orchestra. Not solos, but I have
them in my room, I can pick him out. Though he never
would play here on Sakhalin, even when I found a
flute. Because he had to leave music behind, he said,
to become a musical instrument himself! I have a privately made tape of him playing jazz out on Lake
Baikal in a boat. Friends recorded it. It's so mourn-
ful, that horn across the waters, as though he is sighing
that he will soon slip underwater himself and be re-
born as a water beast. Then music and body will be
one, but then no humans will ever hear him properly
or understand him. Only though our machines and
symbols."

To Richard it sounded very much as though she was
reciting the plot of some Russian ballet. As though she,
too, was playing a part, not perfectly authentic. A
copy, herself, not the original. Maybe there wasn't any
such Russian ballet. Still, the account rang a small
alarm bell in his head. He couldn't take it quite on
trust.

Perhaps it was the fault of telling it in a foreign
language. Perhaps her words would have sounded sin-
cere and unsentimental in Russian. What leeway was
there, after all, for phony romanticism or pretension on
Sakhalin between the cold and the computers? Yet
what a tragic romantic this skinny girl seemed, for all
that, under the functional blue overalls that might have
held a wrench in them, and the heavy military-style
coat. Computer programmer as ballerina! He wondered what the Russian for "soulfulness" was. Probably *sobornost* covered it. Yet he liked her for this, de-

spite his mental quibbles. Whatever else, at least she was fighting to be a real person—no mean feat. So few ways to be real, so many to be unreal.

Ultimately he felt that he trusted her. So he could put up with what sounded like false notes. In her naïve, hurt way, she was utterly charming. Her emotions, still raw and valid. He—though he acknowledged this aspect only briefly—had met someone as emotionally maladroit as himself: who had experienced the shocking, the cruel and the beautiful, and embodied them. So he felt at ease with her. And knew what must happen between them, soon. Never before had he possessed such a clear foreknowledge of precisely how another nervous system would respond to his own, without evasions, without fumbling guesswork.

"Do I sound childish to you?" she inquired suddenly, reading his expression. Her tongue darted out to lick those full, waxed lips, so curiously dry: small red fish, flicking up against a barrier that was melting, melting. "Am I silly? Infatuated?"

"I wish," he hesitated. "I wish I'd been in the position to feel the same. You had *sobornost* with Pavel, didn't you? Now he has it with whales. I feel so envious. I've only been able to stand and watch, from a distance . . . from clifftops . . ."

Her eyes shone. The little red fish had almost melted its way through.

She held up her muddy fingers and placed her palm against his, splaying her fingers and rotating her palm till their two hands composed a star of fingers in the air. Swiveling her hand, she gripped his wrist tightly, and pulled him into the copse. He raised his free hand to ward off the saplings slapping his face, but Katya restrained him.

"Let them stroke you. Shut your eyes so they don't hurt."

So the saplings became caresses, albeit harsh ones.

Then she halted him, to stroke his face with her muddy fingertips and touch the hot marks the twigs had left. He reopened his eyes; quickly, playfully, she whipped off his glasses and hung them on a branch.

"How do you see without them?"

He could see her face quite clearly, in fact. And all the trees. It was distant vision that he was poor on. (So become an astronomer, my son, and harken to the light-years. . . !) Ultimately, perhaps, he wore glasses more as a kind of personal windowpane. Yet, at this moment, he might have been lost in a weedy aquarium tank with her.

"I see a green thought in a green shade," he quoted whimsically. " 'Annihilating all that's made, to a green thought in a green shade.' A seventeenth-century Englishman wrote it. Paul Hammond annihilates all that's made, and leaves us here alone, like this. I guess green thoughts are what whales think under the sea."

So then his tongue searched for the little red fish of hers. And her thick greatcoat made a soft bed for them.

The flesh of his back shivered, exposed to the air, but his chest and belly and thighs were warmed.

Lying wrapped in her coat, with his lighter coat pulled over them, they stared up through spruce branches at a sky glazing over again with impending rain.

"You purr like a cat when you make love," she said.

"That's nice. I think I am . . . what's the word the priests use? . . . unghosted, unhaunted now."

"Exorcized?" Richard spelled it out. "It means 'unghosted.' "

"We made love the last time, Pavel and I, on winter snow out there. A bright blue day, very still. I know that's from a new snowfall, but . . ."

So that was what she'd been probing the snow for. Some crystal imprint, long melted!

"It was the very day before the scanning. He was saying good-bye to his human body, together with me. It was so beautiful, Richard, his last rhythm as a man. But then he got scared when he'd said good-bye, that way. Terrified. He fled through these trees. The branches whipped him to a halt. His eyes wept, blind ..."

"So I'm only his ghost for you."

A great disappointment and disenchantment swept over him.

"Oh, no, not that—*nikagda!* Never" She caught hold of his wrist again and mimicked the Star with their fingers. "See? I'll show you what Pavel is now, when we go back. You'll understand."

As they pulled their clothes on, fumblingly assisting each other, as she might have helped blind Pavel, it occurred to him that people generally said something like this, about the other being bound to understand, when the very thing they feared, and knew positively, was that the other person could never possibly understand, in a thousand years.

Rain mixed with sleet chased them down the slopes to sparse Ozerskiy's huddled smoky houses. Collars turned up, they fled from the thousand stinging darts fired at them from the hills where they'd been lovers.

From those woods where his sperm had acted as the psychic douche for the girl!

Yet as they ran down the valley together, she turned her head and smiled such an open, radiant smile at him that he thought instead: from the place where I set her free ...

He returned her smile. For it's surely something to have set a fellow human being free. Liberation—a revolutionary act! Would that Italian Morelli have any objection to that way of putting it? He'd been the revolutionary lover before a land-mine made him the embittered voyeur of other people's folly.

The squall passed over and out to sea. They shook the water from their coats and hair like otters, before the veranda of a large wooden house; then mounted the steps on to the covered walk. They passed two barred, shuttered windows. The third looked into a gaily decorated nursery. Plastic rockets and space stations hung on elastic from the ceiling. Piled on the wooden tiles were other, apparently functionless toys made out of twisted wire and string, guts of clocks, bent spoons, buttons. A poster painting of Salyut in earth orbit had been half-ripped from the wall. Only the upper, unreachable part still clung there. The missing half was being crumpled and uncrumpled monotonously and expressionlessly by the child sitting bolt upright on his bed. His fingers flexed of their own volition, in and out, in and out. Crumple, uncrumple. Nothing else about him stirred.

Georgi Nilin.

Behind the next window a gaunt shaven-headed figure in striped blue pajamas and a woman's cotton twill dressing gown occupied a bathchair.

His fingers fiddled with his penis through the flaps of the gown, and saliva glistened on his chin. This room was stark and undecorated, though some music was playing from a tape recorder. He betrayed no re-action to the song, except insofar as his head was bent that way.

One song ended, another began. Richard had thought Tchaikowsky or something cultural would have been in order. But no.

"Soviet pop songs," Katya shrugged. "That's Ludmila Zykina now. It doesn't matter what the sound is! We're only afraid if the room is quiet, he'd be so totally alone. Even if he understands nothing, maybe the presence of the noise is a comfort. See—" She pointed, her expression an amalgam of disgust and tenderness. "He is playing with himself, so maybe he's content. Though I doubt he can feel very much sensation. The pain-killing drugs numb him. He didn't look like that before the scanning," she added quickly. "Not . . . when we . . . you know. But he has degenerated since then."

So hard a task to reconstruct the Pavel Chirikov he had once been from that figure in the bathchair! Richard slapped imaginary plasticene on his cheeks and sprouted him a full head of hair. But it didn't work.

The resulting image was merely grotesque. Pavel's immune system even rejected cosmetic repairs—a total immunity, his now: to his body, to the whole world. Starveling idiot beggar in a woman's gown, they left him and returned past Nilin's window, where the boy was still crumpling the poster. It was with a shared sigh of relief that they stood on the drying grass again.

But while they walked toward the main research block, glancing back they noticed a figure appear at an upstairs window of the wooden house, to watch them. . . .

"So they've let him return already!"

"Who?" Richard's glasses were still slightly streaked by rain; vision was wobbly. "He looks familiar."

"Mikhail the attendant! Yes, he *defected* with Nilin, didn't he, Richard?" She laughed bitterly. "What games Orlov plays!"

She shrank inside herself, withdrawing a mental pace or two from him. Her tongue licked nervously. The barrier was back.

"So the defection was a game then? Yet Jonah isn't a game!" He nearly added, "is he?" but stopped himself in time; it would be a fatal remark.

She said nothing. He might as well already have said it. Have cast doubt.

All along, this rusty nail had been waiting to drive itself through their feet and poison their *sobornost*. You couldn't race hand in hand down Russian valleys, carefree as lovers, for long! She must have known this far better than him, he reflected. She'd lived under these conditions all her life.

Kapelka met them as they reentered the main building; nodded to Richard knowingly, or was it sympathetically?

"There shall be another *Zvezdaja Mysl* two days from now," he announced. "Jonah will congregate with the six other whales quite near your San Diego, so you can observe it all. When Jonah is locked in the Star, our trawler transmits the Hammond Theorem to them. To them, through his consciousness. It's being encoded now. Our own government seem just as anxious for a solution, Dr. Kimble! Some dissidents in Eastern Europe ... It's in *Pravda* today."

Tailing off, he touched the girl briefly on the arm. "Pavel will prove himself, Katya! A proud moment."

Twenty-five

They swim through a sea where a Wailing One sings
the warning song describing the Destroyers of Sound,
(Word) and (Hand).

DISRUPTOR is not a true glyph; but a null-glyph, the
first such to be formed. It carries prohibitory inflec-
tions; for it disrupts the clear vibrations of the fluid
universe. With DISRUPTOR there springs up a wall of
razor reefs in the sea of mind, hard and cutting—enclosing no mirror of insight, instead cutting meaning
into the world through the agency of a (steel) instrument . . . This is a mutant growth in the sound womb
—sticking out spiky limbs such as those that all true
fetuses should retract back into the bud, after that
courtesy nod to evolution. Arms with five tiny arms at
their extremities, with five suctionless suckers more
rapacious than any Ten-Arms' suction pads, *lay hands*
not only on things, branding stinging welts on them,
but reach into the mind itself, twisting sound into
(words) tough as (steel) and equally implacable . . .

DISRUPTOR seizes hold of the ever-vibrating waves
whose interactions pattern out the shapes of Being,

and hammers them into (tools) to turn around and
peer at themselves. Those are (words). Those are
(hands). Yet they only measure themselves, describe
their own solid, rigid isolation.

DISRUPTOR, lacking the STOP-inflection, might well
harden oil wax into a glyph that never melts into another greater glyph. A glyph of bone; of stone; of
(steel).

Oh, proto-arms can be heard by his Kind budding
in the wombing mother, while they click-scan her; yes.
Terribly, once or twice, they fail to ungrow again.
Then an awkward, hampered thing is born with meaningless, crippling limbs hanging off it; maybe to drown
right away; maybe to thrash through seas more slowly,
dive less deeply for a shorter life. Lately, more such
buds have been sprouting longer, as queer traces taste
the seas . . .

Tastes put there intentionally by (hands) . . .
they now realize.

His Kind are keenly aware of their own evolution
retold in the wombing; the glyph RECAPITULATOR
pulsed by a Female Star after fertilization is a shape
which the fetus may copy, in growing. A pup begins
life with a glyph of his growth ranging around him,
magic, mimetic, to help him take his proper place in
the evolution toward Greater Glyphs that still lie far
beyond, far away ahead in time.

The glyph REPRESENTOR has raised up the ghost of
another life in another Being-mode. It rose through
the lattice of this one's mind in disconnected drops of
knowledge, to make a waxen dummy; and now he
wants to send a message to someone, to link hands
across the air . . .

But the pulse from the sky, hurling itself willy-nilly
at the Eight-Arms in him till all its arms are dancing,
numbering, has told him- the next Star is critical for
(Humanity).

There is a question, that (hands) and (words) demand an answer to.

His guardian drops behind.

He swims ahead to meet the Two, and the Four.

While the Click-Whistlers hush the Singing Ones, before snuffing their own whistle-chatter into silence . . .

Twenty-six

Once more predictions were rife that the San Andreas
Fault line was about to split open and slide half California into the sea. In many people's minds Hammond's Proof had fatally weakened the bonds of matter: almost as a direct physical consequence of its
pronouncement. The world grew insubstantial and
treacherous around them. Indeed, a series of small
earthquakes—tremblors—nudged the ground beneath
their feet for a week. The Corps of Engineers was
pumping thousands of tons of water into deep porous
rock as part of their Quake Defusing Program, and
small shocks such as these had been foreseen, though
inadequately publicized, perhaps for fear of causing
fear. Now the world seemed to rock on its hinges, and
many people's mental world rocked, too. There were
enough believers—or disbelievers—of an apocalyptic
cast of mind these days, not only to welcome Hammond's Proof (a "proof" now, courtesy of the media)
as vindicating their own manias and anxieties, but to
send tens of thousands of them trooping from the Los
Angeles area and from San Francisco toward Mount

Palomar, as to a sacred place that would not be overwhelmed, imitating the disastrous Mezapico pilgrimage on a vastly greater scale. A millenary movement was under way, in the mind and on the ground. By the time state troopers had sealed off the highways leading to the area, repeating the same mistake as their Mexican counterparts, there were already an estimated fifteen thousand people penned within the area, and perhaps twice that number outside. The official roadblocks and picket lines did not last long, and ended bloodily. . . .

Thus the Hot Days began. Though it was autumn. Perhaps it had seemed the autumn of the world for long enough, with only winter looming ahead, empty of heat and food, work and commodities. Thus people flared up, themselves, to recapture something precious and amorphous: the texture of their lives. Or to commemorate its loss, its gigantic negation.

And this was only in California, where Chloe Patton was once more. She didn't particularly care to know what was happening elsewhere in any other states or countries.

Yet she was perhaps the first person to realize that anything was going wrong out there at sea. . . .

Safe in the refuge of the naval center, marines guarded her—and the installation—from the effects of what news commentators were by now predictably referring to as "the new Hammond Wave," of shock, hysteria. But, from returning sailors—and many simply hadn't come back when the base whistles recalled them—she'd woven a nightmare picture of the frustrations and anxieties being discharged, in and upon the city of San Diego itself: the hippie saturnalia in Balboa Park, the trashing of the El Cortez Hotel by cycle gangs after a college youth playing sniper fired into them from the moving stairway high above the sidewalk, the running battles in the downtown area between gangs and sailors and military people and "American Revolutionaries," erupting through the bars and ballroom dancing schools.

Chloe sought sanctuary, not among the dolphin

pools this time—for they were tainted—but finally in the main telemetry room. Here, signals from the sonobuoys and seabed "ears" scattered over thousands of square miles of Pacific Ocean were being scanned and sorted.

"Hi, Miss Patton, we're just waiting for the word to be passed to your Jonah buddy." The technician waved at the wall clock, which indicated 15:35. "Soon as they get the Star pattern confirmed, the Soviets'll feed the data in. See, here's the Russian trawler—the *Marshal Zhukov.*"

The singing of the trawler's propellers appeared as sharp vertical pips on his cathode-ray screen.

Sixty similar oscilloscopes in the room were devoted to the scrutiny of leaping, slowly fading phosphorescent fleas. The great master oscilloscope, to the right of the clock, was inactive at present. Red lights blinking on a giant glass display map of the Cal-Mex offshore waters responded to whichever buoys or ears the various screens were reading, indicating by their clustering what a mass of hydrophonic gear must have been airdropped into the whale rendezvous zone in the last day. The techs manning the consoles switched frequently from one channel to another hunting around the area. Characteristic signatures of pilot whales, bottlenose dolphins, and a humpback, scribbled themselves briefly on the green screens, were chopped off, to spring up again as one red light on the map died and another blinked alive. No sperm whales, yet.

A tech periodically switched in the sound channel to confirm a particular signal. Chloe heard the characteristic loud smacking of a pilot whale overlaying the footsteps-on-broken-glass noise of the snapping shrimps; then the high wail of the humpback, with the sound of its own bottom-echo mixed in with the song; then the whistling and click-chattering of the dolphins.

It was up to Russians on faraway Sakhalin to encode and decode the signals; but they could keep watch and ward here in San Diego.

"We're all rooting for Jonah, miss," whispered a tech as she trotted from screen to screen, peering in at the leaping squiggles of light.

The commander stood below the wall map, hands clasped behind his back in a disapproving attitude. So Soviets had an agent dressed up in whale flesh, programmed with an ambiguous mission, only a metaphorical stone's throw away from this very spot; and his staff hadn't yet succeeded in pinpointing it, though the Russians had even told them where it should be. He found this personally humiliating, and intended to order an investigation and procedural overhaul.

One of the techs finally turned his audio up confidently, and the room echoed with some unusually sparse clicks from two sperm whales. Judging by the wall map, the sonobuoy floated only a few miles southwest of the *Marshal Zhukov*.

"What the hell are they playing at, sneaking up so quiet?" the commander growled.

"Maybe saving their voices for later on, sir?"

"Don't be facetious, Donaldson. Whales need their sonar, to watch where they're going. You'd better watch out, too! This has hardly been an adequate surveillance operation. We shall have to smarten up."

Resentment replaced the humor in Donaldson's tone.

"At least we've a better notion what whales are up to, than what many of our own people are doing ashore. . . ."

A quartet of sperm whales was detected, off to the northwest of the trawler; finally, a singleton heading in from the west.

"My screen's gone deaf, sir—"

"Mine, too—signal just died—"

The oscillating light tracks had flattened into horizontal wires. A few kinks and quavers still pocked them, though. Fish must be croaking and honking in their usual way. Before Chloe could point this out tactfully, the commander arrived abrasively at the same conclusion.

"The whales and dolphins have all plain shut up,

you idiots!" he marked. "Damned evasive beasts!"

All cetaceans had fallen silent, from the great baleen whale down to the dolphins.

The Star came together fifteen minutes later, three miles from the *Marshal Zhukov*, a quarter-mile from the closest sonobuoy monitor.

The trawler had switched off its engines and was drifting now. It was 16.05 along the western seaboard of the United States.

Abruptly, amplified click-trains and burst-pulses twanged and rattled around the room. Copied onto the master oscilloscope grid, now activated, the signals from the sonobuoy drew themselves in great jagged loops. Seven voices pulsed in parallel, then the composite click-song firmed and speeded up, the loops becoming a broad, glaring, pulsing hand; while the audio broadcast a lacerating, grating groan, that swallowed up all sounds of individual clicks. Some vast slug weighing tons was dragging its way across a stone desert, agonizing with the effort. Such a noise as a glacier might make as it grated its way downhill, accelerated from geological to clock time! This muffled smashing boomed in their ears. Whatever organization it had eluded them: it even jammed the visual display, with a broad band of green light.

The tech wearing headphones to eavesdrop on the trawler's VHF band raised his hand.

"Russians are sending to Jonah now, sir."

No way of telling what difference fresh input made, with the output drowned in that vast gonging, blinding blur. . . .

So this, thought Chloe, is the wisdom of the whales. They've been expounding their own abstract philosophies for how many thousand years: examining the harmonics and dissonances of existence. When we spy on it, even with our finest equipment, it's as solid as the voice of the glacier, or the waterfall. Yet every grain of ice, every atom of water, has special significance for them. . . .

The Russians are listening from their trawler in a

smooth sea, their hydrophones unperturbed by the noises of their own vessel, the ropes grating, hull creaking, jangling cutlery in the galley. Probably they have sonobuoys out in the sea, too. They're faced by the same blank wall of noise. Their own symbolic code, however, dense and elaborate to them, is plaintive plainsong from a different era of the world, as they wait for their loyal Jonah to beam the answer to the Hammond Theorem back to them in a mode that man could understand.

The whole noise output was being taped. It could all be slowed down; computer programs could presumably be written to dissect it. All they could hope for right now was some simple general answer to the question man had posed.

Meanwhile, this great groaning door hinge ground on and on in their ears, without any sign of the door opening. . . .

The Star hung together twelve minutes, till 16:17 Pacific Standard Time.

Total silence, then

The green band shrank abruptly to a single tight bright line neatly bisecting the screen. And this line bored on and on, seemingly frozen, as though time had halted for whales and men alike.

Silence on the smaller screens, too—all those that were reading buoys in a radius of a dozen miles around the Star. Some tiny kinks of fish noise appeared on the left and scurried to the right, and that was all.

Then the master screen came to life again. It wrote out a clear looping pulse. A fast series of clicks rattled in the room. The same shape and sound repeated themselves over and over.

On the cathode tube the clicks resembled a written word, made up entirely of elongated, dipping and soaring *m*'s and *w*'s and *v*'s, traced by a marvelously fluid, rapid hand.

"Is that the answer? What's it say?" someone asked, taken in by the illusion that there was an actual word there, capable of being spoken. A single simple solo word. . .

mwvwm . . .

But they'd all been taken by the same illusion; all been racking their brains to read it. Wishing and willing to make it into a word!

mmvvmmw . . . vvwmvmm . . .

Sporadic laughter greeted the remark—of a nervous, defensive character.

"The answer's got to be a radio message," the tech monitoring the trawler's VHF snapped, shamefacedly. He too had been staring at those loops on the screen, moving his lips, mouthing possible candidate words. "There's no radio message."

"Sir," interrupted Donaldson, "I know that profile. I'm sure that's why it looks familiar. We've seen it before."

Other screens came alive with dancing signals as he spoke, as the noise of this click-train radiated through the waters.

While Donaldson was hunting through a pile of oscilloscope photos, Chloe hurried to the screen she'd last noticed listening in on dolphins. It had lit up with renewed signaling, too, when the soundwaves reached it. She stared, horrified. Then fumbled for the audio control past the operator.

A simple two-part whistle pierced their ears.

The frequency rose up high, then fell off rapidly, to be followed in turn by an ultrasonic squiggle so high that the oscilloscope could trace it only by damping and flattening the signal. The green blip scraped a curve sheer along the grid roof: an exponential function swiveled on its side. High-pass filters cut off the upper ends of this shriek, on audio; nevertheless the speaker spilled sounds into the telemetry room that set metal surfaces resonating, heads aching, stomachs curdling.

The two-part whistle, again.

The high scrape—

Quickly the tech shut off the audio with a twist of his hand.

"It's the dolphin alarm call," Chloe cried. "The S.O.S! Panic stations—! You hear it only when a dolphin's in mortal danger—"

"It sure sounds like it!" the tech agreed, rubbing his ears. "Maybe we ought to play it all over town, scare sense into people."

"No, the alarm's not meant to *scare*, its to bring help. But that's only the whistle on its own. Not that banshee wail at the end—that's never been any part of it."

"Traced it, sir," called Donaldson, flourishing a photo. "Quote. *Physeter* alarm call. But there's something else on the big screen. Miss Patton's right, those last loops aren't here. That's *alarm plus x*—"

"It's trans-species, the alarm call," Chloe added swiftly. "Toothed whales of different species rally to help each other. We knew that even before the Russians told us how the sperm whales can get baleen whales to sing to them. We just didn't realize the extent. . . . Dolphins are passing on the call the sperm whales put out. But it isn't an alarm, only. It's the alarm modified by something else—an extra inflection. It might change the meaning entirely. Did somebody have a humpback on their screen?"

"Cruising about twelve miles west of the trawler, miss. Right now he's quiet."

"He's waiting to pass on the news, the decision, whatever. Watch him. Baleens are stupid as cows, but their songs carry thousands of miles. Their voices are the messenger pigeons of the sperm whale, even if they understand about as much of the message as a pigeon!"

Shortly, the hundred-foot humpback began to sing. They heard a long, wailing eerie music. A message was even now heading out at five thousand feet a second across the Pacific, up towards the Arctic, down south toward Antarctica.

An hour later, the first of the toothed whales came ashore, north of San Diego. . . .

Twenty-seven

They came ashore at Kujirajima, a school of porpoises, a bottlenose whale, even a narwhal with the long twisted unicorn horn. . . .

Exhausted from hours of swimming toward land, they launched themselves on to the lava flow, continuing a parody of swimming as the sea receded, thrusting themselves a few more meters across the black naked honeycomb razors of stone, flensing their skins and blubber, opening rivulets of blood along their undersides.

Waves returned, lapped around them, but couldn't pull them back into the sea. Only their blood flowed back, while their frames settled on the lava, weight of their unbuoyed mass pressing down on their lungs.

It was a heavy-gravity planet for them, with a surface of serrated iron—and they blinked and sighed at the spectators who inhabited it, who were clutching cameras and baseball gloves and painting easels protectively, as though these toys might be confiscated by the strange beasts, in the way that much else had recently been confiscated by circumstances.

Curiously mute, for spectators of such a strange occurrence . . .

It had dawned on the people, that something more *was* being taken off them, which they could do nothing to forestall; namely, these dying porpoises, this bottlenose whale, this narwhal with his miraculous horn. . . .

So they put down their cameras (which really had very little film in them) and their painting sets (with only a few squashed tubes left in them), and tried to lift the bleeding narwhal back into the sea, it being the rarest and strangest of the castaways.

The narwhal stretched the length of three men laid head to toe. Its horn was another man's length. Thousands of kilos it weighed. They only succeeded in sawing its wounds on the lava edges, provoking a low moan from the beast, and freeing fresh streams of blood to mingle with the oily, flotsam-spattered spume. One man stroked its jutting corkscrew, thinking fitfully of the virility charms sold in Chinese chemists' shops along with pickled snakes and salamanders and ginseng roots; then his hand fell away. They retreated sadly from the beast.

They daren't even contemplate the bottlenose whale, with its giant-domed forehead that might have held two brains in it, and that expression of fixed imbecile amiability about the lines of its mouth—no matter what pain it was suffering. Huger than three elephants! With what mania it had levered itself on to land! With what swollen, amiable agony it now lay there, perched absurdly on the rocks.

A man who had raced to the restaurant to telephone some newspaper returned crestfallen; news was already flooding in from a hundred other sources, of similar events.

The restaurant proprietor accompanied him to marvel at such a tonnage of raw whalemeat. Then his heart too sank, for it seemed that this must be the very last banquet of all, laid out before him here on the lava. It spelled bankruptcy, not riches. From the people's faces he knew that no one would compliment him

on any meal made of this, however perfectly prepared,
as freshest *sashimi*. Why, they weren't even trying to
haul the beasts up from the dirty grease of the tideline.
They were actually trying to lift the meat back into
the water—having switched their attempt by now
from the impossible whales to the merely-man-sized
porpoises. They were almost succeeding in manhan-
dling a slippery bleeding torpedo-tube of a body—till
Captain Enozawa ran down the path from the institute.

He'd returned for the ceremonial cups of saké following the funeral of Dr. Kato.

Crisp in his dress uniform, he stopped them.

"I'd set that *iruka* down. It's really no use, what
you're doing. I'm sorry . . . they've tried lifting them
back into the water elsewhere, already. They swim
ashore again. Besides, those are injured. Damaged.
Don't you see, they've committed an honorable *seppuku*, so leave them to bleed. They have no knives to
stab themselves—only the rocks of our shore."

So they set the porpoise gently down, having succeeded only in staining their holiday clothes with
grease and blood; and Enozawa stood there contemplating this sea unicorn, and the massive bottle-
nosed elephant of the ocean next to it; with the rose
blood washing from their wounds.

Had Kato foreseen something of this, when he
wrecked the preserving tanks, and carved his own
body with those wedges of glass? An intuition?

"What makes you call it a *seppuku*, sir?" one fellow
asked—a small-town shopkeeper. Cheap, awkwardly
cut suit; shirt open down to the third button showing
off a smooth ivory chest.

Now, the way Mishima had done it . . . He'd had his
loyal assistant to deliver the quick coup de grace, and
stem the pain. Admittedly there'd been political con-
siderations involved. If Mishima had been rushed to
hospital and his wounds sewn up, he would have been
discredited. Still, he was saved from the full path of
pain. These whales and porpoises had no loyal *kaisha-*

ku man waiting with a sword poised. They simply waited, sighing and looking landward and dying.

"Because it has to be, fellow! When a situation is intolerable! We of all people should understand. . . ."

"Don't whales sometimes run ashore in a panic, sir, by accident?" the shopkeeper asked tentatively.

"Fool! Would you accept the invasion by alien beings of your soul? Beings who were poisoning your world?"

"Invasion, eh? How do you mean, sir?"

"Men have found ways into the minds of the whales."

How could it stay a secret for long, with all these bodies littering the beaches of the world? Oh, scientists might pretend that some heavy-metal pollutant in their nervous systems was responsible—mercury or cadmium had driven them mad! But it would be a pointless lie.

"Well, sir, didn't we Japanese feel much the same when America invaded us?" the shopkeeper observed lamely. "Our soul was breached. And our land has been poisoned since. And we imitate them—" Suddenly the man flushed with rage. He gestured helplessly at the baseball mitt he himself was wearing, some parasitic growth that had infested him—though he'd been pitching to his son across the lava happily enough half an hour ago. Now oil and porpoise blood smeared his glove.

"Poisoned!" he hissed. "Ah, you're right, sir! I believe you when you say it is possible to invade the whales, as America invaded us. If we were to go into the sea, and into the whales themselves—these may have acted correctly. Thank you for explaining, sir."

Flecks of blood flicked off the mitt onto the officer's uniform, as the man tried to rid himself of it.

The porpoise was wearing a glazed look in its eyes by now. A pained exhaustion, that appeared more fine and delicate to Enozawa then any porcelain he had ever admired. Brittle beauty of the pure and agonizing deed. Men must think about all this and reassess their values.

Enozawa bowed summarily, muttering a leavetaking apology which the shopkeeper returned with a hoarse emphatic bark.

As he strode away up the lava spill, for the first time in years, a haiku formed itself spontaneously in his mind, calming and ordering his thoughts . . .

> In a whale's eye
> The glaze of a T'ang bowl—
> Reflected!

Twenty-eight

"So much for Paul's big breakthrough!" smirked Ruth.

Nonetheless she was visibly shaken by the sight of that windrow of corpses littering the strand below the cliffs.

Wild dogs were worrying the sun-high flesh and stinking blubber, which the Mezapico Indians had been hacking at all morning to so little effect, whistling shrilly to each other along the shore in frustration as much as in excitement. That so much should come ashore, after such dearth! It seemed an insult. A malicious joke.

Father Luis said they blamed the telescope. The great mirror had mesmerized the sea.

Ruth recalled Richard Kimble's flippancy, uttered near this very spot, about attempting to whistle whales ashore. It *had* been his flippancy, hadn't it?

Of course it had. She hated the memory of him. His stupid quizzical face. Blinking. Puzzled. Paul had brushed Richard away like a fly as soon as his buzz had become even mildly annoying. Then what did he do but go tamely to feed Paul's devil message

into some computer they'd rigged up out of whales'
brains!

These bodies on the beach were his responsibility,
as surely as if he'd whistled them on shore with his
own fingers stuffed in his mouth. He was guilty
through and through. How she loathed him.

Gianfranco Morelli and the priest stood by her, gazing down.

Finally, Morelli shouted in protest:

"This isn't even real! It's the final damned illusion of
that bastard."

"How do you mean, not real?" Father Luis inquired
incredulously.

"Oh, maybe real for us! But not real for them. No,
not for the whales, the really intelligent ones."

"Unreal for them because they're dead?"

"No, father. Reality branches into so many possible
universes. That is what physics proves. We argued
about this before."

"I remember. But I don't see—"

"The observer chooses his own branch. The result is
the consensus reality we all inhabit. The world as we
see it about us, and far out into space. I suppose only
the mad are excluded from consensus. Even they are
held here physically by the pressure of so many other
minds agreeing on the form reality should take."

"We lock them up," muttered Ruth.

"No! By 'held here' I mean that they don't disap-
pear into alternative mad universes because of the
pressure of everyone else's thoughts upholding this
one. But now we have chosen to embrace Paul Hammond's insane antiuniverse. Chosen passionately and
greedily, to salve our own despair. But the whales—
ah, the whales—they had a choice to make, too."

"They chose the road less traveled by," quoted Ruth
nostalgically, recalling a poem she read in high school.
An allegory of life, the teacher had said. . . .

"No, it is we humans who choose the byroad," Morelli contradicted. "Those chose the highroad of sanity
and a healthy universe."

"You call suicide a sane, healthy pastime?"

"They haven't committed suicide, you little fool! They didn't choose the Hammond branch. They refused it. For them the universe branched a different way. To a positive world."

"For Chrissake what are all those corpses?"

"Ruth, those have subtracted themselves by choosing another reality. Yet we still live in a rational world, it seems, so we have to rationalize their disappearance. They have to seem to die. That is reality for us: their rotting bodies. Truth is, they have escaped. Who knows, from their point of view, but that this whole planet is now purging itself of humanity? Even now in their universe they see us racing into the sea to drown ourselves! They are nosing our bloated bodies around all the coasts of their world!"

Ruth recoiled.

"You've flipped."

"He's a good man, but misguided," Father Luis chided. "The whales really came ashore to help us. They redeem us with their sacrifice. See—"

Laying a frail hand on Ruth's arm, he turned her to face in the direction of San Pedro de la Paz. The upper tiers of the well-icinged church sparkled above tin and tile roofs. And—

"Jesus wept—they've broken through," she whimpered, overcome by a throb of terror, and excitement.

Cars, trucks and bikes were emerging, racing in their direction, toward the cliffs. . . .

"No, Señora Hammond, I imagine the authorities have deliberately let them through. To see this with their own eyes."

Using his hold on her arm to balance himself, he knelt down in a rickety way.

"Now I can pray once more. I feel a clarity in my soul. These creatures are the saints of our day, returning to this land after how many thousand centuries? Precisely when we need them and their death, to restore our souls to us."

"So this is your version of the Second Coming?" sneered Morelli. "God help us, don't you understand, we are left all alone!"

The priest started to cross himself; changed his gesture halfway through, from a cross to a simple fish sign scrawled in the air: twin curves, forming a pointed head at one end, an open tail at the other.

"*Icthús*," he intoned, "was the old private name for Christ. The Greek word for fish. The letters spell out his name—'Jesus Christ, God's Son, Savior,' in Greek . . . do you see? The fish redeems us . . ."

"There's not a fish in sight! They're bloody animals, whales!" The Italian sputtered incoherently; and meanwhile the mob advanced. . . .

"The shape is the same," Father Luis observed blandly, tracing the fish scribble more confidently to right and left, fitting it over the bodies that lay below. "Fish is only a word. A swimmer in the sea. Yes, this is a kind of Second Coming, you're right. How unexpected!" But his beam of joy faded as he had to concentrate on the sheer physical effort of clambering to his feet again. Halfway through the creaky maneuver, Morelli grasped him or he could have slipped to his death over the edge.

"It wasn't really necessary, I would not have fallen, now."

"You'd land on a whale and bounce back up again miraculously," jeered Morelli.

Then the first vehicles were pulling up beside them, disgorging their dusty, tattered passengers. Some with cuts and burns, amateurishly dressed with torn linen. Hard to tell under all this dirt who was peasant, who was bourgeois, who was tourist from over the border. Apart from the vehicle registrations, and styles and ages. Trucks with barred wooden sides, clapped-out Cadillac taxis from the city, dune buggies and VWs: all looked as if they'd driven here through a stony hailstorm. A few bulletholes pocked their doors. Windshields had been shattered.

Then came the gang of Satan's Slaves, revving their chopped hogs to the cliff's very edge, spraying dirt over in bravado. Morelli glanced at them nervously, but they paid no special attention to him; the role of pack leader has devolved upon the epauletted shoulders of a pudgy youth with boils, some missing teeth, and a squashed nose, who plainly didn't recognize Morelli or remember Danny's threat. His epaulettes were plastic tarot cards that fluttered from his shoulders like tiny sprouting wings as he rode.

All along the clifftop, people were gazing down mutely on the Indians trying to flense these whales with ridiculously small sickles and knives. Becoming aware of their silent audience, the Mezapico whistled ever more shrilly along the beaches, and it seemed that the very last breath was squealing out of the recumbent monsters.

"This time," said Father Luis, "Golgotha isn't a hill. The crucifixion is on the seashore. See how they all ignore the hill and the telescope? Though they fought tooth and nail to reach it, they've forgotten it. This is the greatest wonder. So I say yes, the whales have redeemed us. Tell me—" He addressed the nearest spectator, who happened to be wearing long hair, with a torn orange caftan flapping open from heavily belted jeans and tanned shirt. "Why did the soldiers say they let you come?"

The American hippie wouldn't take his eyes off the bodies on the beach.

Father Luis asked a second man, wearing a dirty business suit, the tie torn open at his neck, somehow without dislodging his paste jewelry tiepin. But he said nothing either.

The third man he asked was a peasant wrapped in a dingy ochre sarape. This one replied in a vague, hypnotized tone:

"Why, to see the whales walk on the land, father. They say it is happening all over the earth, since we told lies about the stars. So they came out to see for themselves."

Contemptuously Morelli spat down the cliff. His spittle vanished into thin air; the gesture went unnoticed.

Father Luis traced the sign of the fish with two powerful sweeps of his index finger.

"Those are our intercessors," he exlpained to the

man, "who intercede for us with Him. This is a miracle, this thing which men's eyes witness today across the world—to bring faith back amongst us. . . ."

"It's a bloody ambiguous miracle," mocked Morelli. *"Carnage."*

"Aren't miracles all essentially ambiguous, my friend? Miracles represent a suspension of natural law; they can hardly be cut and dried."

"But faith in what, father?" inquired the peasant cautiously.

"Faith in reality! Those have sacrificed their reality so that we can believe in this world once more, and care about her. Our world."

The plump Satan's Slave had been scudding his bike closer in silence with his boots, during this exchange, listening.

Producing a pack of tarot cards out of his leather jacket, he slapped it face down on his fuel tank.

"Choose," he challenged Father Luis.

The priest regarded the cards dubiously, then gestured at the beach.

"What need is there? Our fortune is told."

"I'll pick a card," Morelli volunteered. Before the Slave could agree or disagree, he had whipped a card out of the center of the pack and flipped it over.

The Page of Cups.

The picture showed a man holding a chalice out of which a fish reared up into the air to inspect his face. Behind the man lapped ocean waves . . .

The Angel gazed at it a long while. Then he wrenched the Devil cards from his shoulders and flipped them out over the cliff. Two bright plastic pictures rotored down like sycamore seeds till the void of air swallowed them as totally as it swallowed Morelli's gob of spit.

The plump boy pulled a tattered interpretation manual from his top pocket and thumbed through to the Page of Cups.

"Listen to this. News, a message is what it means. So you're right on the ball, priest, that's our message all spelled out."

Some bodies, dwarfed by height, were still immense enough; particularly one sperm whale corpse. The Mezapico were toy matchstick creatures, by comparison.

Morelli snatched the tarot manual away from the Angel. His face darkened as he read it.

"Liar! You listen to me. You read only part of this. It says also 'it is the pictures of the mind taking form.' And if it's facing you the card signifies a true message, but if it's reversed—and I chose the card, and it doesn't face me!—then it signifies artifice and deception. It means a phony message. A lie."

He tossed the grubby little book down on the ground, for the fat boy to retrieve. His finger stabbed the air.

"*Those* are only images of the mind. They seem real —cut them and they bleed—but they aren't real toothed whales. Those have extracted themselves from this reality of ours. They branched elsewhere. Those bodies are all just phony rationalizations: ways of explaining to ourselves how the whales can have disappeared into a non-Hammond universe! Lies made visible! Mankind's collective hallucination!"

The Angel was attempting to slot the fish card into a tuck of leather on his shoulder.

"Man," he growled, "are you *crazy!* Are you fucking nuts!"

Gently, baptismally, Father Luis helped secure the card to the boy's jacket with a safety pin, produced from somewhere in his robes, mumbling a few words in Latin.

The Italian turned and trudged away from the entranced crowd, heading in the direction of Mezapico Mountain, out across the desert . . .

Ruth waited a while, till he had walked a couple of hundred yards, then climbed into the Sierra and drove after him.

"Want a ride, Gianfranco?"

She coasted alongside him, while he marched obsessively onward, ignoring her.

"Gianfranco! What are you going to do?"

Cactus scraped the flanks of the station wagon . . .

He halted so abruptly that she drove right past him, missed his reply, and had to back up.

"I suppose, kill him," he repeated.

"If you walk all the way there, you'll be too tired for anything," Ruth said amiably. "So hop in."

"Do you have a tool kit?"

"I guess."

"Lug wrench? Jack handle? Pickax—that's how they got Trotsky."

She nodded uncertainly.

"Have to be one of those, then."

He fixed her with a lopsided grin.

"Okay? No objections?"

By the time they got back to the observatory, though, Dr. Paul had already flown out, bound for the Andes. Consuela handed Ruth a hastily scribbled message from her husband, telling her to follow on with Alice. . . .

Soldiers lounged about the base of the Big Dish.

As soon as Morelli, in a fury, started hurling parts of the Sierra's tool kit up at the vultures perched on the spars, they moved over and arrested him.

Ruth departed to pack a suitcase for herself and baby.

In her room, bed littered with clothes, she reread Paul's note thoughtfully.

Ruth—

I'll be working at the Andes Dish for six months. We're fixing it so that Max takes over the daily running of this place. Hire a couple more staff. I'll still be director *in absentia*. Life should be calmer higher up in the hills.

You've been under strain lately. Me too. Bad influences—need I enumerate? Kimble. Morelli. If you feel you need a rest, Ruth, Max can arrange a clinic in Oakland for a time—I'll look after Ally till you're calmer. It might do you good. On the other hand, if you feel up to it, follow on. Your choice.

This note's a bit of a rush—Max can fill you in—

I'm being ushered off the premises by a full col-
onel! The powers-that-be find my continued presence somewhat corrosive, it seems.

Bests,
Paul.

Yes, she would follow on, damn him. Into the even
higher, emptier Andes.

There was a brief postscript . . .

"P.S. Pity the whales took it so hard. We must
have really blown their fuses!

Twenty-nine

Orlov dumped the latest Telex reports on Kapelka's desk, then lounged against the wall: a spiv on a street corner, his coat dragged around him against the draught. The seats were taken by Katya Tarsky, Richard Kimble, Tom Winterburn. Herb Flynn was away examining Sakhalin's first beached whale, which had come ashore on the other peninsula, at Ul'yanovskoye.

Kapelka dreamed briefly of a quiet appointment counting the remaining sturgeon in Lake Baikal, calmly attending at the bedside of the dying. . . . Alternatively, the authorities might leave him here, in this surly spot, on a reduced budget, scribbling fisheries reports. . . .

Yet again, who knows, maybe this whale disaster served some arcane purpose of the politicians? So that he might after all find himself occupying a prestige appointment at the Science City of Academgorodok, as he'd always hoped, carrying on his work of modeling minds. True, there was no other intelligent species to map the model onto, now, except the human one.

Maybe, one day, in outer space . . .

Still, the dog might leap either way.

"Well?" he sighed at Orlov. "So it goes on?"

"Still coming ashore. Africa. Australia. South America, all over. None of the toothed whales will be left alive in a few days apart from a few captive dolphins. The only reason it isn't over already seems to be the distances some of them are having to travel to reach any land. Why don't the Gadarene swine just dive and drown themselves?"

"They must wish us to see?" conjectured Kapelka. "No news from Jonah, Katya? He may know why this is?"

A silly question. She would have told him immediately.

"We *have* tried very hard," Katya replied stiffly. "It would have pained him not to answer."

Such an alien death, for an alien motive, she thought. So soon after the transcendence of the Thought Star, to destroy himself! What was the meaning?

"He must have been one of the first ashore," she said. "Somewhere in California. The panic radiated from the Star he was in."

"Such mindless panic," muttered Kapelka. "And yet, who are we to say it was mindless? When it obviously took the highest intellectual ferment to arrive at it! The baleen whales still scoop up krill and plow the seas like grazing cows, broadcasting this same song around the planet till every last toothed whale hears it. Would we humans act thus on a song?"

Orlov, from his street corner, whistled some bars of The Internationale."

"I guess," Tom Winterburn suggested soberly, "we might commit group suicide with bombs or biological weapons. But never all of us singly and individually by choice. This song doesn't just stir emotions like 'The Internationale' or 'The Marseillaise.' It mimics reality. It's a—what d'you call it, professor?—a mantra of some new, fearfully compulsive knowledge."

"But knowledge of what?" Kapelka demanded. "Of the universe as viewed by this man Hammond? I very much fear it was simply their first true knowledge of *us*—of this race they share the planet with: Humanity, no less. Suppose that you were a Jew trapped in Nazi Germany—"

"I should fight!" snapped Orlov.

"If you were a blind Jew? If you only knew how to sing?"

"I should emigrate. To propagandize."

"If you had no hands to climb the wire fences? Only a sudden blinding vision came of the Nazi *handymen*?"

"We've spent a full century slaughtering cachalots, comrade. They haven't tried committing suicide before!"

"Maybe they didn't interpret our actions the way we would? Maybe they thought we'd grow out of it? I don't know. But what we finally did do, through our Jonah, is found a way of showing the exact nature of our minds to them." Kapelka gestured at the pile of Telex reports from coastlines of the world. "The result—"

Richard urged: "We can rebuild the dolphin population. There must be hundreds scattered around in marine zoos. Even if we can't do anything about the sperm whales."

Katya shook her head vehemently.

"The dolphins will all hear the death-mantra, soon or late, it'll go on being sung forever. That's the last message of the whales. Their singing cows will haunt the seas with it. . . ."

"You become a prophetess, little girl," rumbled Orlov.

"For Chrissake, can't we stop these whales?" Richard exclaimed in frustration. "They haven't all come ashore yet. Can't we herd them back to the open sea somehow?"

"You want to herd the Gadarene swine?" Kapelka laughed brittlely.

"Far too easy to equate this with the Gadarene swine," Katya scowled. "Many people will try to

equate the two events, to soothe their consciences—
especially if the human race learns anything from this.
It may seem that our madness has conveniently passed
over into them. We may feel exorcized. We will not
be. Dostoevsky's *Possessed* begins with those Gadarene swine. But those pigs weren't aware why their
deaths happened. The man Stavrogin in that book
was. The whales are." She glared defiantly around the
room.

"Dostoevsky is politically confused—a mystical reac-
tionary," shrugged Orlov.

"This is getting us nowhere!" Richard seized hold of
Tom Winterburn's arm. "We must be able to herd
whales, Tom! You must know, surely we've got some
ultrasonic scaring machines? Or could we harpoon
them with anesthetic darts?"

"Covering every coastline in the world, Richard?
Within a matter of hours? Talk sense, man."

"Besides," added Kapelka, "*narkos*—anesthetics—
it makes whales and dolphins die, unless you take
great care. They must retain conscious control of their
breathing. We had difficulty with this while we were
mapping the model onto Jonah."

"They'll kill themselves whatever you do!" cried
Katya. "They've chosen their silken cord, as Stavrogin
did to hang himself, and strung it right around the
world, and that cord's made out of a song! You'd need
to stop every baleen whale in the sea from singing."

"Why can't we fill the water with other sounds! Jam
the song as we jam a radio broadcast!"

Winterburn smiled pityingly.

"And how many weeks would that take?"

Kapelka protested: "Anyway, how do we know
what this jamming may do to the baleen whales? Drive
them all mad, perhaps! Then we should see the real
giants coming ashore: the blues and finbacks. Dinosaurs would be puny dwarfs to them. That's five per-
cent of the total protein content in the sea. We dare
not risk it. At the moment, those are still grazing safely."

"We do nothing at all?"

"It's *their choice*, Richard," protested Katya. "Don't you see? It's Pavel's choice!"

"Pavel is some creature in that house over there." Richard jerked his thumb angrily at the sanatorium building. Images of the mind-cripple wearing striped pajamas interposed between him and the Russian girl, impenetrable as a row of bars.

"It's his requiem they're singing in the sea."

"You're haunted again. You always will be, Katya," he said sadly.

"I always will be," she echoed. "Every one of us always will. So the baleen whales shall go on singing their song through the oceans. All our ships and submarines shall always hear it. We shall remember. Yet never really understand."

As they sat staring at the veranda of the house, the hunched figure in the wheelchair was pushed out, by Mikhail, to soak up a late autumn patch of sunshine.

About the Author

IAN WATSON is the author of *The Embedding*, which in 1974 was nominated for the John W. Campbell Memorial Award. Born in England in 1943, he graduated from Oxford with a First in English, then went on to do research in comparative literature. He has taught at universities in Africa and Japan and has published stories and articles in a number of magazines.

OUT OF THIS WORLD!

That's the only way to describe Bantam's great series of science-fiction classics. These space-age thrillers are filled with terror, fancy and adventure and written by America's most renowned writers of science fiction. Welcome to outer space and have a good trip!